BEWITCHED IN DARKNESS

A PARANORMAL WITCHES & SHIFTER ROMANCE

JEN KATEMI

Bewitched in Darkness (Hellhound Protectors)
Copyright © 2021 Jen Katemi

ISBN 13: 978-0-6451898-3-4

Print Edition
Published by Flourish Books (Jen Katemi)
Cover design by Jacqueline Sweet
Edited by Rainy Kaye

CONTENTS

Sapphire

NOT EVERYONE GOES demon-hunting to prove to their family they can look after themselves, but I guess my circumstances are a little different to the average twenty-five-year-old. Though I can't believe it has come to this—time to say goodbye to Amethyst and Topaz and head out on my own.

The fallen angel Azriel is in my sights, and I have the beginnings of a plan to bring him down.

Despite the insistent pounding of my heart and the guilt churning in my stomach, I know I'm doing the right thing. Whatever misgivings I have about keeping Ammie and Tee out of the bigger picture have to be shoved down into the dark place deep inside.

It kills me that I can't tell my sister and cousin—my two best friends—more about what I've been up to, and what I'm planning. But I know how *that* revelation will go. I've been through it before, and both of them still see me as the little one.

The immature, out-of-control one.

The one who needs containing and protecting.

Usually that thought makes me chuckle, but lately, I've been getting frustrated. As much as I love them both, I can't afford to have them freak out on me like they've done so many times in the past.

There's no time for the inevitable arguments or justifications. In their mind, I'll always be the baby of our family of three, and it will always be their job to protect me from the big bad world if they can.

Not this time.

I'm tired of hiding the extent of my power and pretending to be something I'm not.

In this situation, where we're up against a fallen angel and his demon minions and we've exhausted pretty much every option that Amethyst or Topaz can think of, it is time to embrace who I am and step up to adulthood once and for all.

This time, I'm going to take my place as an equal in our coven.

And that means I need to go it alone.

My mind wanders back to the other night, before Ammie and Dane returned from the Accord Headquarters. I sat in my suite of rooms at the Aurora Spa Resort, cross-legged on the floor, as I tried to meditate to calm my stress levels.

As usual, I sank down into the mire of darkness that sits somewhere deep inside me, searching for peace. My magical powers originate there, in the dark space within my soul, and every time I use magic, it feels as if the shadows grow, just that little bit more.

The voice came out of nowhere, reverberating all around me.

Embrace the darkness, Sapphire, in order to reach the light.

"What?" I jumped to my feet and spun, but there was no one else in the room. Was it Azriel or one of his demons returning to finish the job? "Who are you?"

Be true to yourself, Sapphire. Embrace the darkness, and the light.

"Ah... okay?" I wrapped my arms around my middle, willing my frantic heart rate to slow. This was supposed to be meditation time, intended for relaxation, not "scare the bejesus out of Sapphire" time.

Laughter rippled through the air, and with it, the caress of what felt like fingers on my hair.

We are not of the dark, child. We will be there to guide you, when you are ready.

There was no more after that. I sat back down and tried to re-enter my previous meditative state so I could continue the conversation, but the voice remained silent.

I wasn't sure what had happened, but since then I haven't been able to stop thinking about the mysterious voice, even during the clash with Azriel and his demons two nights ago.

I'm sure he didn't notice me on the battlefield—he was so clearly focused on Amethyst, the one who had reached out for him in her dream state and called him to the resort.

It was then that the beginnings of my plan took hold in my mind. If I have guidance—possibly of the celestial kind— then perhaps I can explore the darkness further, in the form of trying to get closer to Azriel, knowing there is someone or something to guide me back toward the light.

The resort took a real beating from the battle. Trees and shrubs were uprooted everywhere, and large gouges of earth mark the places where various skirmishes took place. The worst of the blood and gore and mess is gone, thanks to Kyan and Dane's shifter pack members doing some of the heavier grunt work and starting the clean-up.

There's still a bit of effort required to get the resort back to decent, but at least the wards are up once again, and stronger than ever thanks to the three of us combining our magic to reinforce them.

Ammie has decided to stay here for now, guarded by Dane

and a couple of shifters, but Topaz said she'll return with Kyan to his pack lands, which are equally well-protected thanks to the magic left there by my mother and aunt many years ago. Tee should be safe enough there. For now.

There is no doubt in my mind that Azriel will be back, either in person or via one of his demon lieutenants like Luthor. They still want Topaz's soul, but now they also want Ammie's and mine, as well.

They won't get them.

Not if I can help it.

And now I have a nebulous idea of how we might be able to stop their murderous hunt.

We are not of the dark.

Perhaps I can use that knowledge to help save my family.

I'm startled from my thoughts by the sound of distant voices approaching through the trees. Kyan and Topaz appear, hand in hand. They are so happy together, a perfect pair, as are Amethyst and Dane.

A bite of jealousy runs through me, but I tamp it down. I'm strong and independent, and perfectly capable of living a happy life without a man by my side.

If we survive the demons, that is.

Kyan raises his hand in greeting, and I do the same. He and Topaz have agreed to give me a ride home, and reluctantly promised not to tell Amethyst about my plans to leave, until it's too late for her to stop me.

Hence my guilt. I don't want to leave my sister without saying goodbye, but it's time.

"Ready to go?" I call out.

Topaz's eyes flicker and she turns to Kyan. "We're all packed. Not that we brought much."

She glances behind her, toward the edge of the clearing, where the smoldering remnants of a huge bonfire remain. Dead hellhound bodies, demon wraith pieces of clothing—in fact, any debris left by the Otherworld army—have been gathered up by various members of Kyan's pack, and thrown into the magic-fueled fire. All of it is now nothing but harmless ash.

"Ammie," Topaz says. "Do you think she'll be—"

"She'll be fine," Kyan cuts in. "Dane is in charge of the clean-up, and he won't stop till everything is exactly how Amethyst wants it."

Topaz looks at me, and I nod encouragingly. "Kyan's right. She'll be fine here, for the next little while. As you will be, if you return to Ky's pack territory."

"You saw that?"

"I did."

Knowing is one of my specialties. I just know things others don't. Things that other people walk right past, unaware of the potential danger that lurks just around the corner.

Some might call it a gift. Not me.

Most of the time, it's nothing I can't handle. A strange buzzing in my eardrums if a supernatural creature brushes by me in a bar, or a shiver down my back if a vampire crosses my garden late at night. Or if I get one of my premonitions that something bad is about to happen, then I might experience a sick feeling in my gut.

Annoying, but inconsequential.

But other times? It's a *nightmare*.

Being around lots of people makes the knowing so much worse, especially when those people are human and I have to tamp down my magical abilities. Everyone's emotions—the excitement, anxiety, jealousy, fear, sadness—suck at my energy until I can't keep my shields up, and I worry all the time that I might inadvertently hurt someone if I lose control.

I made it a grand total of four days at college before the frenzy of campus life drove me into a total meltdown. By the time I called Amethyst and she came to pick me up, I was a wreck.

It wasn't the first time that happened, nor the last.

Goddess, it's no wonder Tee and Ammie look on me as a baby. I haven't coped very well with what others consider "normal" life, up to now.

The ability to know things isn't constant, of course, as magic is not an exact science and is never guaranteed to appear on call. But in this moment, I'm telling Topaz the truth. I did see hers and Ammie's relative safety, at least for the next few days, and she knows me well enough to believe me.

Her face relaxes a notch. "Okay. Then let's get going."

ONCE WE'RE on the road, I heave a sigh of relief. I'm at least one step closer to finally making my own path in life. Despite the ever-present danger, my spirits lift.

Ammie tries her best, but she doesn't understand. Not really. Her powers are neat, organized, and self-disciplined, just like her. Well, her crazy dream walking with Azriel notwithstanding.

And as for Topaz...

I sharpen my gaze on my cousin in the front seat. She has the window rolled down, one pale hand resting on the sill, the other gently curved on the top of Kyan's thigh while he drives. I can't see her face, only her long dark hair waving gently in the breeze.

She defied death itself. Things don't get much more powerful than that.

What's happening now, with Topaz and Amethyst being stalked by a fallen angel, isn't something that *anyone* can ignore, not even me.

And my "knowing" ability only makes things worse.

It doesn't matter where I go, or what I do. I can't escape the bone-deep dread that lingers inside me. The certainty that haunts my every waking hour—that the situation with our fallen angel demon stalker is about to get a whole lot worse.

2

As we leave sight of the resort, Topaz twists in her seat and spears me with an intent look. "So, what are your plans now, Sapph, after we drop you home?"

Kyan's eyes catch mine in the rear-view mirror. He is listening but seems content to leave the conversation to us.

"Would you rather come back to Kyan's pack lands with us?" she asks. "*I'd* prefer that, if you don't mind. At least then I'd know—"

"Actually..." I cut her off, before staring down at my hands, forcing them to relax in my lap. When I raise my head, I feign a casual attitude, like I haven't been thinking about this—*planning* this—for days. "I'm going off the grid again."

"Off-grid, as in home, to your place? Or, into hiding?"

Technically, my home isn't off-grid. It is just situated in a small community where there are less people, and the atmosphere is quiet.

"Home," I confirm.

Somewhere I can try to tap in to whoever spoke to me the night I was meditating.

Kyan frowns at me through the mirror. "Are you sure? Hiding might not be a bad idea..."

"No." I cut him off before he can say anything more. "I have an idea that I want to explore."

I hold up my hand as Topaz's eyes widen. She's readying to argue.

"I can't elaborate at the moment, but I promise I'll share when I can. I'm thinking there might be a way to get close to Azriel. He has supporters around him, yes? Followers?"

Kyan and Topaz exchange a glance. Both of them look concerned.

"I guess so," Kyan says. "Most of the hellhound shifter packs still serve Otherworld masters."

"But not all," Topaz says gently, giving his arm a squeeze. "What's this about, Sapph? What are you planning?"

I quirk a grin at her. My cousin can read me well; I will have to tread carefully.

"What if I could find a way to get to him from the inside? What if I could get into his inner circle, and gather information that way?"

I'm not even sure where the idea has sprung from. All I know is, since that night when the voice appeared, the thought of tapping into my own darkness has grown.

Did the voice mean, approach the enemy? Look the darkest of the dark—Azriel himself—directly in the eye? And in doing so, maybe I can find my way back to the light? If I can get home, and reconnect with the being that spoke to me, maybe I can clarify that point, plus a few other things.

Topaz's face turns aghast. "What? No!"

Surprisingly, a thoughtful expression crosses Kyan's features. He drums his fingers against the steering wheel. "Funny you should mention that..."

"What the fuck, Ky!" Topaz's eyes flash at him before she turns on me. "Do you have any idea how dangerous—how *insane*—that would be? We all almost died because of Azriel, and now you want to walk into the belly of the beast, and... what? Offer yourself up as a sacrifice?"

"Don't be ridiculous." I slump back in my seat and cross my arms, resisting the urge to roll my eyes at her dramatic tone. "Believe it or not, I have thought this through."

"Well, clearly you haven't," she snaps. "Because if you think I'll let you do this—"

"*Let* me?" I lean forward, tugging on my seatbelt impatiently when it locks. "I'm not asking for your permission."

"Then what are you asking for? Approval?"

"Actually, I asked you for a ride." My voice is stiff. Will they ever see me as an adult? "Kyan, if you pull over, I'll make my own way from here, thanks."

"Enough!" Kyan says. "Topaz, I know you're worried about Sapphire—"

"I am," she says. My annoyance fades at the genuine fear lacing her voice. "I'm sorry, Sapph. I'm just... so scared. For all of us."

"I know. I'm sorry too, cuz."

She shoots me a wobbly grin.

"I think I might be able to help you with an in, Sapphire," Kyan says.

"An in?"

"Yeah." He reaches one hand across and links his fingers with Topaz. "Don't be mad, Tee, okay? Hear me out."

"I'm not mad. I'm scared the people I love are going to die. And I feel powerless to stop it happening."

"Sweetie," I start, feeling like the grown-up in the group, for maybe the first time ever. "We're in danger right now. In this car, in the city, on the beach, at the resort... it doesn't matter where we are. Not really. There's nowhere safe for us anymore. As long as Azriel is hunting us, we'll *never* be safe. Doing nothing likely means we all die anyway. So, I have to do something. I have an idea, but first, how about we listen to what Ky has to say, and then take it from there?"

She releases a short laugh. "When did you grow up, Sapph?"

I grin at her, relieved the last trace of discomfort between us is gone. "A long time ago. You and Ammie just didn't notice."

Kyan clears his throat. "Right, then. So, nothing we can say will change your mind?"

My heart starts racing. "Nope."

Nothing short of locking me up. And even then, I'll probably just use the quiet time to reach into the dark and try out my idea, anyway.

"I have... someone I've recently been in contact with," Kyan says. He sounds like he's weighing each word carefully before he speaks. "Someone from my past, who I trust as much as a pack brother. He might be able to get you in."

I'm too shocked to answer. Of all the things I expected him to say, it wasn't that.

Topaz lets out a huff. "Ky..."

He flicks a glance her way. "Sapphire is old enough to make her own decisions. At least this way, she'll have someone to look out for her. Trust me, okay? This guy... he'll protect her. I swear it."

Topaz's brows pinch together. She doesn't look happy, but eventually she gives him a tight nod.

Kyan's hand returns to the steering wheel. He glances back at me through the mirror. "I'll take you to him, under one condition. *Do not* ditch him to go running off on your own."

"A babysitter? Great, thanks."

"You don't know the Otherworld, Sapphire. Any army commanded by a fallen angel, headed by demon lieutenants..." Kyan shakes his head. "There are things I've seen that you wouldn't believe. Think of him more as a partner, okay? You both have different skills, different specialties. I think you two will get along like a house on fire."

My mouth twists. I want to say *no, thanks,* but there's a bigger picture here. If this guy can get me close to Azriel's inner circle, he might be the ticket to figuring out a way to destroy the fallen angel once and for all.

I can't afford to miss this chance.

Trust your instinct. This is the right decision.

"Fine," I mumble. "I promise I won't ditch the babysitter."

I only hope the babysitter doesn't turn on me. Or end up betraying us all.

3

WE PULL over for a few minutes while Kyan exits the vehicle and makes a call. The silence in the car as Topaz and I watch him pace back and forth, gesticulating every so often with his other hand, is both awkward and comforting. I know Topaz cares, and her over-protective attitude toward me stems from love rather than anything negative.

It is still a relief when Kyan returns, his presence breaking through the awkwardness.

"He'll meet us further up the road. Somewhere secluded," he says, before starting the car and heading off once again.

Instead of sticking to the main highway, he turns onto a secondary, smaller road, driving us further east, in a loop back toward the forest. My trepidation grows as the trees thicken around us. Their branches reach skyward and the shadows lengthen as the road narrows sharply, turning to dirt before twisting and weaving around dozens of blind corners.

The sense of something dark pressing in on us rises. Where the heck are we headed?

My pulse rate increases the further into the forest we go.

You wanted to tap into the darkness, I tell myself. *Stop being a baby and suck it up. Can't be that much farther.*

"Are we almost there?" Topaz echoes my thoughts, peering out of her window. She keeps darting nervous glances back at me, clearly not happy about this turn of events.

"We need to meet my contact somewhere private," Kyan explains. "Sapphire's right—nowhere is truly safe. But there are a few places where we are less likely to be... overheard."

We head deeper into the shadowed forest, until I can't see an inch of sky anymore, only thick foliage. By the time the car rumbles to a halt, the track is uneven beneath the wheels and the air is still and silent.

I push open the door and hop out, inhaling the forest air gratefully. It was a long car ride, longer than I expected. Despite the sense of oppression surrounding us, the cool freshness of the breeze is bliss. I reach out and brush my fingers along the fronds of a nearby fern. It curls up at my touch.

Even the shadows seem strange here; a deep, inky blue that creeps out from the undergrowth.

Where are we?

I take a seat on a nearby log as Topaz and Kyan converse in low voices. Kyan makes another brief phone call, then comes to sit beside me.

"Just confirmed. He's on his way." He rests his elbows on his knees.

A prickle of frustration runs down my spine. "How far away is he? *Who* is he? Does he have a car? Does he have—"

"Hey, come on." Kyan holds up his hands, laughing, and I snap my mouth shut. "He's someone I know and trust. He's in the area already, doing reconnaissance to make sure we're alone. Relax, he'll be here soon."

Maybe. Or have we just walked into the biggest set-up in history?

I want to trust Kyan. I *do* trust him, when it comes to my cousin. I know he'd turn the world over if it meant keeping Topaz safe. But he's a hellhound, originally from the Otherworld and answering to a demon master, and I can't help but worry that he might have misjudged something this time. A lot has changed since Kyan and his pack left their old lives behind.

For one thing, Topaz *died*. And then the Fae brought her back. Somehow, that act upset the balance of energies in the world and allowed rifts to appear in the ether. Demons have risen, and now a fallen angel wants to seize this world for his own.

Maybe Kyan *was* friends with this guy, once upon a time. But who knows where the proposed babysitter's loyalties lie, now?

Despite Kyan's casual insistence, I can't relax. I sit here, my knees jittering beneath my deceptively calm hands, refusing the snacks that Topaz brought for the trip, despite one of them being my favorite—salted caramel popcorn.

There's a change in the air around us. It's almost imperceptible at first, but it grows and grows, causing all the tiny hairs on the back of my neck to rise up and prickle in a warning.

A rumble vibrates the earth beneath my feet, becoming louder and louder, until the invasive sound tears through the trees. I leap to my feet, eyes wide, as a giant man on an equally giant black motorcycle roars into the clearing and pulls up in front of us.

Topaz's slack jaw reflects the same astonishment as my own, but Kyan doesn't look surprised. He wanders over to the bike as its owner switches off the engine.

Silence fills the space. Kyan slaps the new arrival on the back.

"Caden!" he says loudly. "Good to see you, man."

The figure astride the motorcycle is clad in black leather. His helmet is shiny, its visor reflecting the trees around us, obscuring his face. When he pulls off the helmet and shakes out his almost shoulder-length dark hair, my breath catches in my throat.

Holy guacamole. Now that's *a babysitter.*

I nudge Tee, holding in a nervous giggle, and she releases her breath in a whoosh as we stare at Caden.

There's no mistaking him for anything but a hellhound shifter, even in the gloomy light of the forest. His black hair, sharp jawline, and cheekbones mirror those of both Kyan and Dane, and those brilliant green eyes are unmistakeable. They are the only thing about him that flare with any kind of emotion. The rest of his features might as well be set in stone.

Undeterred by his friend's impassive façade, Kyan grins widely and claps a hand on the man's shoulder. "Thanks for getting here so fast. We don't have long."

He glances around us, like we're already being hunted.

Maybe we are.

"Come on, I'll introduce you."

Topaz and I linger awkwardly a few feet away from the two men. The motorcycle between them glimmers, its clean metallic lines standing out against the dark trees behind it. I swallow heavily as the man swings a leg over the bike to dismount and turns his gaze toward us.

Something strange flutters in my belly.

Must be nerves.

Kyan holds out a hand, gesturing for us to come closer. I steel myself and take a few steps forward, trying to ignore my racing heart and act nonchalant.

What is wrong with me? I've met dozens of shifters in the past few weeks. None like this one, perhaps, but still... I need to calm down.

"This is my mate, Topaz." Kyan slides an arm around Topaz's waist and draws her into his side, before pointing at me. "And this is her cousin, Sapphire."

Mentally, I shake my head, annoyed with my reaction to the newcomer, and stick out my hand, determinedly making eye contact. "Pleased to meet you."

He regards me without giving anything away. My cheeks heat as he tilts his head to the side and looks me up and down. He doesn't take my hand, instead leaving it hanging.

Great. So, he's an asshole.

I lower my hand, before clenching my fingers and releasing them. The strange prickling sensation over my skin intensifies, as if I'm having some kind of weird allergic reaction to his proximity.

Kyan clears his throat, no doubt sensing the awkwardness. "This is Caden. He'll be your..." He pauses and I know he nearly blurted out the word, *babysitter*. Instead, he changes tack. "He's agreed to help you find a way in to the fallen's inner circle."

The fallen? Are we not saying his name anymore?

Out of the corner of my eye, I catch Topaz's incredulous glance at Kyan. She seems as skeptical as me, about the strong-yet-silent Caden.

Without warning, he reaches out and fastens his fingers around my wrist. My jaw drops as he tugs me toward the bike, and I dig my heels firmly into the earth.

His head whips around. He actually looks *surprised* that I'm not about to submit to being dragged onto the back of a motorbike by a total stranger, without a word being said.

Surprised, and annoyed.

Well, that makes two of us, pal.

"Every second we spend out here, we risk discovery." *So, he can speak.* Caden's voice is low and gravelly, conveying no emotion whatsoever, save for a vague annoyance. "It's time to leave."

"Yes, I agree," I say. "But—"

"Is there a problem?" Caden regards me with a look reserved for a child throwing a temper tantrum. It does nothing to soothe my surging anger.

"Not at all," I reply, through gritted teeth. "But I would appreciate a few of your precious seconds to say goodbye to my cousin. I don't know when we'll see each other again. Or even if I will."

We stare at each other for a long moment. Eventually, he gives a curt nod. His fingers loosen around my wrist, and I slip out of his grasp and launch myself into Topaz's arms. She wraps me in a tight hug, and I blink back the sudden moisture in my eyes.

"Be good," she whispers to me. "Don't do anything stupid, okay?"

I chuckle and draw back far enough to look her in the eye. "What's that supposed to mean?"

"It means," she says, tucking a stray piece of my hair back behind my ear, and all of a sudden, I'm six years old again, "Amethyst would literally murder me if I didn't make you *promise*."

Her eyes glimmer, and I realize I'm not the only one holding back tears.

"So just... keep safe, okay?"

I find myself nodding and give her a shaky smile. I can't promise anything, but it seems to be enough for her.

My gaze drops to the ring on her left hand, the one that features a topaz stone. It glows softly in the forest shadows.

"You don't happen to have any spare warding charms, or power boosters, do you?" I point at her ring, only half-joking. "You know, just in case?"

She looks taken aback. "Sapphire... you don't need

anything to enhance your powers," she says. "Other than that warding charm around your neck."

I clutch at the silver chain necklace and lift the deep red pendant stone that sits just above my cleavage.

"Why a ruby?" I ask. "I always wondered why you didn't make me a sapphire charm."

She grins at me, clearly glad to be on familiar ground. "They're the same family, you know. Rubies and sapphires. They just have a different mineral mix. And with this one..." She flicks the stone with her forefinger. "You don't need anything else, hun. Even though Ammie and I have always tended to baby you, we know you're the most powerful one of the three of us. Like the sapphire and the ruby. Same family, different energy mix. We just don't like to acknowledge it, I guess."

I gape at her. The admission is completely unexpected.

"Now go. If Ky trusts him..." she says, lifting her chin toward the shifter and his motorbike, "then we should, too. Be safe, cousin. Please."

I barely have time to tell her I will, before Caden is huffing and puffing at my side.

"We have to leave. Now." His gruff voice sends a shiver down my spine. I roll my eyes to hide the reaction.

"I better follow my orders," I mutter to Topaz. "Wish me luck."

"Oh, Sapphire." Topaz's eyes twinkle with amusement. "I'm not sure if I should be wishing *you* good luck, or Caden."

4

RIDING on the back of a motorbike is not what I expected.

We fly through the forest at a dizzying speed. The trees are a dark blur around me, and the wind whips through my clothes.

For a wild moment, I don't feel like myself. I feel like some other girl, a girl I could never truly be. Easy-going and fun, like Topaz in the days before she almost lost her life. Like any of those vibrant, laughing non-magical girls that flocked through the corridors at college.

They were the ones I envied; the ones who always seemed ready to hop on the back of some guy's bike on a whim. They were the ones whose lives seemed like one big adventure to someone like me. I've always lived on the fringes of life, because of my often-uncontrolled magic. I hovered outside of society, looking in.

Free. For the first time in my life, I feel free.

Surely, even a fallen angel intent on destruction could not catch us while we career through the countryside this fast?

I relax my death-grip around Caden's waist once the track widens out, and the hairpin curves and bends give way to a straighter road. I'm certain he already thinks I'm some kind of fragile flower, and I don't want to give him any more ammunition.

Goddess only knows what Kyan told him in that phone conversation.

Caden pulls the bike over to the side of the road. The rest stop is nothing to write home about—it is little more than a ditch surrounded by a few rocks, and a couple of sparse, straggling trees, and a toilet block. We've long ago left the forest behind us. It has to be late afternoon, going by the position of the sun in the sky, and my stomach is regretting that I didn't take Topaz up on her offer of snacks earlier in the day.

The bike rumbles to a stop and I slide off, grateful for a chance to stretch my legs and arch my aching back.

The stop also provides a chance to gather my thoughts.

The Sapphire who hugged her cousin goodbye in that clearing is gone. I left her behind when I climbed onto the bike and conjured up a spare helmet for myself.

This is a new world. I can't trust anyone, least of all the man standing a few feet away, searching for something in the bike's storage compartment. He's not looking at me, but I can tell he's still... watching, tracking my every movement, even with his back turned.

The hyper-awareness that seems to work both ways is an unsettling feeling, and I can't help the shiver that runs through me.

Caden's gruff, monosyllabic voice interrupts my train of thought.

"Here."

"Here what?" I stare blankly at the small metal canister he holds out.

When I don't move, he releases a huff of impatience and moves a couple of steps closer. It's a water flask.

"Oh, okay, thanks."

I realize I'm parched, and knock back several grateful gulps before handing the flask back. He eyes me as he takes a few sips himself, and I try not to fidget under the unrelenting gaze.

"Do you need a comfort break?" he asks, pointing at the toilet block.

I shrug. "Sure."

"Be quick."

Goddess, this guy really has no inherent charm whatsoever. "I'll do my best."

My sarcastic tone seems to have no effect. When I return, he hands me a candy bar. He already has a half-eaten one in his hand.

"We can get something better to eat when we get there, but this should tide you over till then."

"Okay. So, where is 'there', exactly?"

He gives me a look. I didn't really expect him to answer, so I shrug and unwrap the bar. I bite into it gratefully. I'm not sure if Kyan told him about my sweet tooth, or if he just happened to have chocolate in his bike storage.

The latter probably. I can't imagine him stopping off anywhere on the way to meet us, just to get me some sweet snacks.

One candy bar proves inadequate to fill the hole in my belly. I reach in to the shadows deep inside me and ignite a spark of magic.

"What's your favorite snack?" I ask him.

"Huh?" He blinks at me.

"*Quick*!" I can't resist echoing his earlier command. I snap my fingers for good measure, and one of his brows rises up.

"Chicken nuggets."

I wasn't expecting that. "Here you go, then."

I wave my hand, releasing a burst of magic, and a box of

bite-sized hot chicken pieces materializes in my palm. I hand it to him and create a bag of hot and salty fries for myself.

"He wolfs down the chicken. "Thanks. They tasted like real food."

A laugh bubbles up my throat and out.

"It *was* real food. As are these." I hold up the fries, then busy myself filling my mouth with deliciousness. When the fries are gone, I create a napkin and dab at my lips. "So, where *are* we going, Caden?"

Still no answer. He just holds out a hand for the empty wrappers. When I hand them over, he crushes them into one ball and lobs it over his shoulder without even looking— straight into the trash can a few feet away.

Was that a lucky accident, or...

"Score," he says quietly, and flashes me a grin.

I'm so nonplussed, I can't speak for a minute. When he smiles like that, losing the deadpan expression, he transforms from brooding hulk to straight-out sexy dude.

I swallow, barely resisting the urge to flap my hand in front of my suddenly heated face.

"Why did you agree to help me?" I ask, trying to distract from thoughts of his attractiveness.

I think of Kyan, of the phone call he made. The certainty in his eyes when he told me about his trust in Caden. For him to ride all the way out here to pick up a total stranger, even under normal circumstances, was a lot to ask of anyone.

And these are *not* normal circumstances.

Caden seems to comprehend my meaning well enough. He takes a moment to pack away the flasks before he answers. His long fingers make quick work of the fastener on the storage compartment.

"Because we want the same thing."

I stare at him. "Oh yeah? What's that?"

He turns to face me fully. His green eyes are as brilliant as ever, but there's a flintiness to them I didn't notice before; an intensity that has me all but transfixed.

"To stop Azriel," he states calmly.

I wasn't even sure if he knew about Azriel, until this moment. But clearly, Caden has no problem saying the fallen angel's name out loud.

"To end this while there is still the faintest chance we might succeed," he adds.

The *faintest* chance? I bite back the sudden hysteria that bubbles up. Bizarrely, I want to giggle. *Oh, well. When you put it like that...*

He waits, watching me. Like he expects me to fall at his feet or something.

The thought is unfair, but it has been a long day and I've had enough of being treated like Caden is the savior who has zoomed in on his motorbike to rescue me.

I've faced demons, hellhounds... hell's bells, I've fought Azriel himself.

Well, kind of. I've fought in his general vicinity, against his minions, and that has to count for something.

I draw myself up to my full five-foot eight-inch height and tilt up my chin, spearing him with what I hope is a determined and confident look. "Kyan seems to think you can help me do that. Why? What can you offer that I don't have?"

Casually, I draw on the power in the growing shadows around us, dragging energy to me, feeding the darkness tucked deep down in my soul, until my whole body pulses with magic. Conversely, instead of showing as darkness, my magic lights us both in a blaze of silver-white.

It has always been that way. The more I draw on the darkness, within and without, the more my magic lights me up like a Christmas tree.

He blinks and his mouth drops open slightly. I grin,

enjoying the stab of satisfaction that shards through me. I love that I've just caught him off guard.

Slowly, I release the energy, allowing it to trickle back to where it came from, until I'm simply Sapphire once again, standing in front of him without any sign of my magic showing through.

His eyes rake over me with a new awareness, and something dormant deep inside my belly sparks to life beneath his scrutiny.

"I belong to Azriel's security detail," Caden says into the silence.

I take a step back and clutch at my pendant necklace.

"Kyan didn't tell me that."

Should I recall the magic and slay him now, before he gets in first?

Caden's eyes crinkle at the corners in one of his rare grins. "Clearly."

He doesn't look like the enemy, until his smile disappears again.

Kyan trusts him. I say it in my mind, over and over. *And if Caden wanted you dead, he'd have shoved you off the bike around one of those clifftop bends.*

"And yet, you wish to stop him?" I ask, curious.

"Yes. I do."

"Right." Anxiety swirls through me, together with a flare of excitement. This has possibility, definitely. More so than my idea to infiltrate via some nebulous celestial-guided path through the darkness.

"I am one of the Otherworld's most trusted hellhounds, which is why I was assigned to the fallen angel's guard. I can access information that would be impossible for an outsider to obtain. And I can get you in."

I raise an eyebrow. "If you're so close to him, then why do you want to bring him down?"

I cross my arms over my chest, narrowing my gaze, ready to defend the moment he attacks.

Caden's eyes harden, a swirl of crimson flaring briefly. His whole face shutters, like a door slamming in my face, and I know that I've somehow stepped across a line.

And yet, it's a valid question.

"I'm not close to him. I work for him."

There's a difference? He doesn't answer the actual question, I notice.

"You and I are now on a mission, Sapphire." The sound of my name from his lips sends a strange frisson across my skin, one I'm not sure I like. "You can trust me with the mission, and with your life. Beyond that, the less you know, the better."

He turns away, toward the motorbike, and shoves his helmet back onto his head before straddling the machine. The conversation is clearly over.

My lips press together. I don't like to be kept in the dark. My instincts are screaming at me to push further, to force him to tell me everything he knows. But at this moment, it would be pointless.

He seems even more stubborn than me, if that is possible.

If Caden is telling the truth, then like it or not, he does offer a way into Azriel's inner circle. If I piss him off too much, there's no telling what might happen.

Getting abandoned in the middle of nowhere by an aggravated hellhound who works for a fallen celestial could really put a dent in my plans.

"Fine." I grab my helmet and shove it down onto my head. "But you're going to have to tell me something. Soon. I have no idea what I'm walking into. I'm a witch—not to mention one of Azriel's most wanted. What's my cover?"

I catch a flash of humor on his face before he snaps down

his visor. It's the barest hint of emotion, but the unexpectedness of it makes my pulse race.

"A lone human woman in the middle of a hellhound pack." Caden snorts to himself. "You'll never fly under the radar. The best I can do is offer you some measure of protection with a story that seems believable to the others."

The bike rumbles to life beneath us. My thighs tighten around the seat, and my hands reluctantly creep once more around his waist. There is something very intimate about pressing up against a firm male body, while a piece of machinery vibrates between your legs.

"What story do you suggest, then?"

"I'll inform the pack that I've met someone."

"Seriously?" My voice is breathless, and I squirm, trying to find a position where my vibrating privates are not quite so tightly pressed against Caden's rear.

He kicks the stand to fold it away and we roll out of the rest stop and onto the road. He turns his head, shouting over the rev of the engine. "And then I'll introduce you as my new girlfriend."

5

AFTER A FEW MINUTES on the road to think about his suggestion to pose as a couple, I manage to calm down from my impending freak-out. I have to admit that it's actually a neat solution. Probably the *only* solution that makes sense in a short timeframe. Not that I would ever give Caden the satisfaction of admitting that out loud.

Still, the thought of pretending to be his girlfriend sends a shiver of unease through me. Caden and I haven't exactly hit it off so far, and now he wants us to act like we're in love—or at the bare minimum, in lust? In front of his entire pack, and whoever else is hanging around on the fringes of Azriel's circle?

I'm not sure I'm *that* good of an actress.

Goddess, Sapphire. It won't be for long, and it's only to keep up appearances. It's not like he's asking you to marry him!

The voice in my head sounds suspiciously like Amethyst. It's judgmental and a little snippy. It makes me smile, and then a fierce longing for my sister rushes through me.

I wonder if she's mad that I left without saying a proper goodbye.

As the sky above us darkens fully, we approach the outskirts of a small village. It looks faintly familiar. This isn't my own community, but I recognize it as being not that far from where I live. We must have done a big circle and approached from a different direction.

My eyelids have begun to grow heavy, and it is becoming harder to remain alert enough to hang on to Caden's body. I'm relieved when he turns off the main road and slows down near a small jumble of single-story houses and buildings.

I all but stagger off the back of the motorbike. Mercifully, Caden doesn't comment; he merely unbolts the door to the nearest building and steers the bike inside. At a loss for what else to do, I follow him into the dusty, dimly lit space.

"Where are we?" The sound of my voice seems too loud. Too intrusive. I bite down on my bottom lip, trying to quell my racing heart.

Caden dusts off his hands and shoves them into his pockets before turning to me. "My place."

He brushes past me on his way out.

As answers go, it isn't very informative, but then, what's new? I'm beginning to realize Caden is a shifter of few words.

If this is Caden's place, then his pack lands must be situated close by. And that possibly means Azriel's lair is somewhere in the local vicinity, too.

I'm not sure how I feel about that. I never knew a pack associated with the Otherworld was within spitting distance of my own private little community. The illusion of finding safety at home was obviously just that—an illusion.

He strides off in the direction of one of the larger barns. As I race to catch up with him, I take in the faded wooden slats of the buildings around us, and the rough dirt track underfoot that runs between the buildings. This appears to be a farm. Or at least, it once was. I can't see any machinery, nor is there any sign of animals or crops. Just a handful of cars and trucks parked around the place, along with a few motor-bikes. I catch a glimpse through an open barn door of another car with its doors off. The space is lit by a single, yellow bulb, dangling from the ceiling. A pair of legs in greasy, beat-up jeans poke out from underneath the chassis of the vehicle.

Caden stops in the entrance to the barn and thuds a fist against the side of the door frame. "Up and at 'em, Patrick."

The legs jerk, then a man slides out from underneath the car. He sits up, wipes a hand over his graying beard, and scrambles up. The crow's feet around his eyes deepen as he spies Caden and breaks into a grin.

"You've been gone a while."

"Had to take care of some things," Caden says easily, step-ping inside and clapping the man on the shoulder. "How is she?"

Patrick casts a dark look at the car. "She'll pull through. She's given me the run-around today, though. You were right. Her undercarriage has been fucked six ways to Sunday since before you... ah..." He pauses, seeming to notice me for the first time. His cheeks darken, and he wipes his hands on his shirt and shoves one of them out in my direction. "I apologize for the colorful language, ma'am. I didn't see you there."

I take his hand and return his warm smile, relieved that Caden's cold front doesn't appear to be inherent in other members of his pack, if that's who this person is. "Please, don't stop on my account. I've heard a lot worse than that, believe me."

Patrick chuckles. His eyes dart over to Caden, who belat-edly steps forward and slides an arm around my waist. I force myself to relax under his touch rather than flinch and jump away as my instincts cry out to do.

"This is Sapph—Sophie." I glance up at Caden, but he

continues as if undeterred. "She's not delicate, nor a lady, trust me."

My brows rise up. *Wow.* Nice way to introduce a girlfriend.

"Pleased to meet you, Sophie." Patrick's eyes twinkle in my direction. He doesn't seem to pick up on any awkwardness between the two of us, though I'm sure he doesn't miss my nudge into Caden's ribs. "Been a while since Caden brought a girl home."

"I can well believe that," I say, with a sweet smile.

Caden tenses, but Patrick just throws back his head and lets out a bark of laughter.

"You've got yourself a feisty one there, man."

"Don't I know it," Caden says through gritted teeth.

Hmm. So, this is going well. We are so convincing as a loved-up couple.

"It's been a long day," Caden says. "I'm—we're—going to turn in. Just lock up out here when you're done."

"Don't do anything I wouldn't do!" Patrick calls out, as Caden steers me away from the barn entrance and forces me to fall into step beside him. My face is on fire as the sound of Patrick's laughter fades into the distance.

Caden's gaze cuts sharply down at me as we take a right turn toward a sprawling house with a wide porch and a low, sloped roof. Unlike the outbuildings, the house looks neat and well-kept.

"You'll blow our cover if you're not careful," he says in a low voice as we climb the stairs to the front door.

"You started it!" I hiss. "You basically just called me a whore in front of your packmate!"

Caden's arm drops from around my waist like he's been burned. He takes a step back, frowning down at me. "That was... No, I didn't!"

I jab a finger into his chest. "Yes, you did. I'm not a *lady*?

Is that how you introduce all your girlfriends?" I shake my head. "Why am I not surprised?"

"I didn't mean... well, I don't..." His cheeks flush, and his scowl deepens, as if he knows I'm right and doesn't want to admit it.

It occurs to me in a flash of irony how we must look to any outside observer. Standing inches apart, hurling accusations on the porch of his house, we could be any ordinary couple having an argument after an evening out.

Caden's eyes flash, and before I can say anything further, he wrenches down the doorhandle and bundles me inside. I barely have time to glance around the dark entrance hall before his hands are on my shoulders and he pushes me up against the now-closed door.

"Sapphire." His voice is barely more than a whisper in the vicinity of my ear. I want to turn my head away, but I'm frozen to the spot. The heat of his body against mine is a huge distraction. Are all shifters this hot... literally and figuratively?

I blink, realizing that he's talking, and try to re-focus on his voice.

"We have to *sell* this," he says. "If we're not on the same page, things are going to get messy real fast. My pack... it isn't like Kyan's. Some members are still in service to Otherworld masters—*demon* masters, Sapphire—and not all of them want to get out, like I do."

He gestures toward the window to the left of the door. "Patrick, out there, is one of the harmless ones. He enjoys tinkering on the cars that others bring in for repair. I let him use some of the outbuildings as his garage, and in return, he has my back. But not all of the pack are like him. Do you understand?"

My shoulders slump against the door. I might not like it, but he *does* have a valid point.

"Yes, I understand." I glance up. "But Caden, if you want to sell this, then you have to give more back than monosyllabic answers, manhandling, and a disrespectful attitude toward me. I do have some self-respect, you know. And even though this is a fake relationship, there's no way I'm going to let you treat me badly. *That* wouldn't be realistic. Do *you* understand?"

After a beat of silence, he nods. "Yeah. I understand."

"Okay, good." I smile up into his brooding face. "Then let's do this."

Caden

THE LOGICAL, rational part of me wishes I'd never agreed to this stupid idea of Kyan's, to help the witch get inside Azriel's inner circle. What was I thinking, to say yes to such a harebrained scheme?

The other part of me knows that this might be my only real chance to finally get out from under the thrall of darkness that our pack has lived in, for far too long.

Not only me, but some of the others as well, like Patrick.

Freedom seems like a vague and nebulous dream, for most of us, but with the Redferne witches to help us, and the ongoing support of Kyan and his pack if we assist them, we might be one step closer to achieving independence for whichever pack members want to stay with me and start a new life here in this realm.

The fact that the prickly witch I've agreed to protect is one hot and sultry package, is a bonus I wasn't expecting.

My dick has remained in a permanent half-hard-on since the moment Sapphire wrapped her arms around me on that motorbike. When she snuggled up against my back on the ride home, it was all I could do not to pull over to the verge, lift her up and over onto my lap, and let nature take its course.

Every time she moves, her scent drifts upward into my nostrils and sets my nerve endings on edge.

I'm going to have to take matters into my own hands real soon. Or find a cold shower in which to douse my ardor. The ache in my groin is becoming too persistent to ignore.

But first, we need to talk. I show her into the living room, pointing to one of the couches, and take the armchair in front of the fireplace. I grab the knitted throw blanket from the back of the chair and toss it across to her. She wraps the blanket around her shoulders and settles back with a faint shiver.

"Want me to start a fire?" I ask. "It'll take a few minutes to grab the wood from outside, and then we can talk."

She sits forward, and a tentative smile lifts her wide lips. *God, those lips.* As soon as I saw them, all I wanted to do was kiss them.

"Want *me* to start a fire instead?" she says. "It'll take about five seconds to have a roaring blaze right there."

She points at the empty fireplace, and I raise my brows. "Sure. Show me what you got."

Her head tilts, and she flicks a wrist. Just like that, a whole stack of logs appears in the fireplace, and a healthy crackling blaze bursts into life in the hearth.

Whoa. I didn't even see a hint of magic flare then. But the result speaks for itself.

"Okay. Not bad."

"Not bad? How about this?" She waves her hand again, and platters of food appear on the coffee table between us—meats and cheeses, pickles and olives, crusty bread, and one plate piled high with strawberry tarts, and a side dish of cream. "So, are you hungry?"

"Ah, yeah." Now that she mentions it, I realize I'm starving. "There do appear to be some advantages to dating a witch, then."

She chuckles, then we both sober. I pile up a plate with food and then watch her do the same. "You won't be able to do that here, after tonight. Magic, I mean. You're going to be human, and non-magical, remember?"

The light that lifted her features from attractive to beautiful, fizzles out, and I feel strangely guilty for reminding her why she's here.

"I know," she says softly. "I was just... well, I guess I was showing off, a little."

I take a huge bite of ham and bread roll and chew. Who knew magical food would taste even better than the real thing?

"And I appreciate it," I say at last, equally softly. This whole situation is going to be strange for her, and I have to remember that. "But now it's time to talk. We need to get our stories straight."

"All right." She nibbles at cheese and crackers, before crunching down on a piece of carrot. She then takes a sip of iced tea from one of the mugs that appeared with the platters. "What is our story?"

"How did we meet?" I ask.

She slips off her boots, then tucks her legs underneath her. She looks so comfortable in my living room—so much at home—that I have to work hard to focus on our conversation.

"You came into my jewelry shop a couple of months ago to buy your mom a birthday present," she says.

"You run a jewelry shop?"

"I *own* a jewelry shop," she corrects. "Design my own pieces. Topaz uses some of them to create charms for her clients, at times."

I file that information away to consider later and shake my head. "That's not gonna work. Mom's dead. Next?"

"Oh, I'm so sorry. I—"

I raise a hand, cutting her off. The last thing I want is pity —from anyone, but for some reason, particularly from Sapphire.

"It was a long time ago. I can barely remember her."

"Hmm. Well, if that's designed to reduce my pity, it actually has the opposite effect."

I shift uncomfortably, not sure what to say. I'm not used to entertaining women who want to actually talk. Most times, it's my body and my bed they want. Or my body and the kitchen table. Or the back of a car. Or...

"Okay," she says, interrupting my train of thought. I can see her curiosity has been piqued, but she manages to contain it. "Then you came to my yoga class one day, and we hit it off."

"Yoga?"

She throws up her hands. "Fine! Why don't *you* come up with an idea, then?"

I study her, concocting and discarding one idea after the other. She folds her arms across her chest and stares back at me with a mulish cast to her features.

Finally, an idea sticks. "There was a border dispute between two warring shifter packs about a month ago."

"Uh huh. And?"

I lean back, regarding her carefully. "And you wandered into the middle of it one night without realizing you were on shifter territory. I saved you from being torn apart by an angry shifter. You were *very* grateful."

She laughs, a merry tinkling sound that sends an unexpected shiver across my skin. "Yeah, no. That would never happen."

"Why not?"

"Because I'm a kick-ass witch well capable of saving herself. I don't need *you* to rescue me. It's most likely to be the other way around."

I shove food in my mouth to stop from swearing. This woman is more cantankerous than... well... *me.*

When I regain control of my temper, I sit forward on the chair.

"You're not a kick-ass witch."

Her eyes flash and she opens her mouth, but I hold up a hand to cut her off.

"You are *Sophie.* A normal, non-magical human woman who, until recently—when I *saved* you—has had no contact with the supernatural world."

Her mouth snaps shut, and eventually she sags back against the couch. "Fucking hell. You really do seem to bring out the worst in me, Caden. But I will try and play along, from now on. You savior of innocent witches, you."

Spare me from stubborn women! "You need to do more than try and play along." *Your life will depend on it.*

I don't say that last part out loud, but she's already aware. A desperate glint appears in her eyes. From what Kyan told me, Sapphire and her coven sisters have faced a whole lot of danger in the past few days. If she was really stupid enough to think the danger is over, then she and the others would already be dead.

She's clearly not stupid.

And she can obviously hold her own.

Luckily for me, I wasn't at the battle on the beach, nor at Sapphire's sister's resort. Otherwise, I may have been on the opposing side—not by choice, but because I haven't yet found a way to officially free our pack from the machinations of the Otherworld.

Instead, I was off in the mountains gathering information about the Summer Fae, for Azriel. He is concerned about the rumblings of war among some of the immortals here on earth, and he wants to get ahead of anything that might have the chance to upset his plans.

"So, I need to hero-worship you, as my rescuer?"

I shoot her a quick look, ready to be annoyed, but the amusement curving up her lips stays my bad mood. I can't pin down how to categorize her; she keeps changing and I can't quite keep up.

"Yeah, sounds good to me." I decide to go with humor myself. Might as well try and enjoy this situation, as much as possible. "Plus, my sexual prowess. You definitely worship that."

"Hmm. Now that might be a step too far," she says, but her grin has widened, and I find myself relaxing, for the first time since I met her. "But we do have a lot to talk about, Caden."

"Agreed. We need to do it tonight, because the rest of the pack will likely be all over you come tomorrow. Now that Patrick's met you, the word will spread fast. We need to convince them you have no supernatural ties."

She nods, looking thoughtful. "Sophie," she says softly, then repeats the name out loud. "My name is Sophie Wintergreen."

My mouth curves up. "Wintergreen?"

She shrugs, and a hint of pink flares in her cheeks. "There was a girl once, when I was a kid, in one of the foster families we stayed with. I kind of had a little crush on her—you know, one of those innocent six-year-old crushes. She had the palest golden hair and blue eyes, and she always had the prettiest dresses in the neighborhood. I wanted to *be* her. Normal and full of light and joy. Her surname was Wintergreen."

For some reason, the hint from her past warms me, right down deep in my core. I have no idea why, but a gentle rumble rises up from my chest in response.

"Hello, Sophie Wintergreen." I lean across the table and extend my hand. "It's really good to meet you."

As I enfold her hand in mine, a flare of anxiety shards my chest.

She is heading into a situation that could well end in death, for her and for me. Somehow, I have to navigate a path that keeps both of us safe from Azriel, and at this moment, I have no idea how to do that.

6

Sapphire

THE MOMENT I lean over and our fingers entwine, something changes between us.

I can't quite identify what it is. Maybe it's because it's the first time we've properly touched, skin to skin, except when he has tried to manhandle me. Maybe it is the lingering reminder of his hard body between my legs as we rode that cursedly seductive and always-vibrating motorcycle. Maybe it is simply the heat in his expression every time he glances my way.

This is *fake*. I'm not really his girlfriend, and he's nothing like Kyan or Dane, who obviously care so deeply for Topaz and Amethyst, and likely did so from the moment they met.

Not that I was there for either of my coven sisters' first meetings with their mates, but from the "gaga" look in every-body's eyes, the relationships have progressed to serious at warp speed for both my sister and my cousin.

This shifter sitting in front of me is very different. He has not extricated himself from the Otherworld, and he works for the enemy. Literally. He is nothing like any other hell-hound I've met. Hell, he is not like any other male creature of *any* species I've ever met.

Caden is rougher, less polished, than the shifters in Kyan's pack, and by his own admission, has worked closely with a fallen angel who wants to bring down civilization as I know it.

He is not of Kyan's pack, and yet, Kyan still seems to trust him enough to put my life in his hands.

Should *I* trust Caden, too?

Is there something deeper in this man? Something I'm not seeing on the surface, that appears to be singing out to my instincts to trust him?

Trust the darkness, Sapphire. It will lead you on the path toward the light.

The angel's voice keeps reverberating in my head—if indeed, it was an angel that I heard. Is *Caden* the darkness I need to trust?

I thought the voice was referring to the darkness within myself.

Everything about this goddamn hellhound shifter sends my senses into overdrive and my brain into a tailspin. His huge fingers curve around my hand, dwarfing it with his, and I have to fight the urge not to jump over the coffee table and climb into his lap.

Not a good start. We need conversation, not—

"May I kiss you, Sophie?"

"Ah, what?" I blink at him, wondering if I look as stunned as I feel.

"We should have some familiarity with each other, before tomorrow, don't you think? Physical familiarity, I mean. If we don't..."

He trails off, but I get his drift. "You think, if we don't, the others will somehow know?"

"I believe so. Shifter senses are finely honed. Our scents are not yet... mingled."

"All right."

Jeez, I couldn't have waited even a few seconds more, before I blurted that out?

Caden doesn't seem to notice my eagerness, or if he does, he doesn't remark on it. He stands, pulling at my hand and drawing me to my feet.

"Come here, Sophie." He guides me around the coffee table. "I very much want to taste that beautifully wide and incredibly sexy-looking mouth of yours."

The wide and sexy mouth in question drops open, but before I can formulate a response, he drags me in against his body and lowers his head, claiming my lips with his own.

Holy mother. My brain switches off, and all I can do is feel.

I think my hands end up in his hair, and one of us moans deeply when his arms tighten around me and we mold together from head to toe. No idea whose moan it is. I can't tell where he ends and I begin. The kiss is practiced, open-mouthed, and completely overwhelming as his tongue pushes in and claims me in a way I've never been claimed before.

Heat and sensation explode in my mouth. And not just there, but everywhere. The connection blasts down my veins, as if his essence permeates my very blood, sending ripples of need right through my whole body before the desire pools between my legs.

Without a doubt, this is the hottest first kiss I've ever had.

Eventually, somehow, I manage to break away from him. I feel as if I will lose myself completely if I don't. He releases me instantly and I stumble backwards, knocking the back of my legs against the edge of the coffee table and taking a few deep breaths to try and clear my spinning head.

What the hell just happened?

How is it possible for one person to have such an all-consuming effect on another like this?

When I raise my gaze to his, he looks about as dazed as I feel, and a tiny part of me is grateful I'm not the only one who feels as if I've just staggered off a particularly dangerous roller coaster ride.

He raises a hand to his lips and rubs them, as if wondering what we just did, before folding himself back into the armchair in a loose-limbed movement.

I sidle around the table and collapse down onto the couch, and stare into the flames of magically created fire in the grate because it is easier than staring at him.

I'd forgotten all about the fire, but luckily, the logs won't need any poking to keep the flames burning bright. Magic will keep it alive, as long as I choose.

Unlike the relationship between Caden and me, a traitorous voice whispers in my head. Magic and the supernatural might have brought us together, in a weird way, but now I need to deny my magic altogether, if we are to have any chance of surviving this situation.

"So, ah..." I clear my throat, almost afraid to ask. Afraid of the possible answer. "Are our scents... *mingled* enough now, do you think?"

He huffs out a breath that is almost a laugh. "I believe so."

"Okay, good." I fold my arms across my middle, still looking at the fire. "It's been a long day. Where should I—"

"You can sleep in my room."

I look up at that, and Caden's eyes bore into mine.

Will you be sleeping there, too? I swallow, once again feeling pinned to the spot by the force of his gaze. I can't quite bring myself to ask.

He frowns, as if aware of my sudden misgivings. "Azriel's spies are everywhere. Anyone could be watching. It's the way he maintains his hold over us... rewarding those who are loyal to him."

I think about Patrick's friendly smile. It seems unimaginable that a man like that would betray me to a demon. And yet, there was a watchfulness in his eyes...

I shudder. "What happens to those who aren't loyal?"

Caden's mouth tightens to a thin line. "He feeds his demon wraiths with the flesh of those who are disloyal to the cause."

A strong shiver traverses my body, with goose bumps rising up all over my skin. I don't even know how to respond to that comment.

"I guess we'd better put on a good show, then." I keep my voice light, but I'm sure he hears the slightly hysterical edge.

"I always do." Caden's voice is lower than it was before. Even from this distance, I can almost feel the words resonating through my chest.

Thoughts of demon wraiths feeding on dead shifters disappear out of my head, replaced by images of Caden taking my mouth with his. I moisten my bottom lip with my tongue, and Caden's eyes track the movement. There's a hunger in his gaze that scares me, but equally, it ignites an answering hunger in me.

What is wrong with me? We've only just kissed, and I can't get thoughts of doing it again out of my head.

One moment, I'm considering death and destruction and bodies being ripped apart by sharp and unyielding teeth, and the next, I can't stop imagining what it would be like if we explored more of this strange physical connection.

He stands in one smooth motion. I quickly follow suit. He still towers over me, of course, but there's nothing I can do about that, short of standing on the coffee table.

From up there, I could grab hold of his broad shoulders far more easily...

"I'll show you to the bedroom." Caden's voice interrupts my wandering train of thought.

"Great, thank you."

I follow him back into the narrow hallway, glad he isn't looking at my hot cheeks.

While we've been eating and talking, the light outside has faded, giving way to a dark sky studded with tiny stars. To my surprise, Caden doesn't reach for a standard light switch; instead, he twists a knob on the side of the wall, and a row of small lamps flicker to life. The dim light throws deep shadows against the wall before flaring up and casting his face in a warm glow.

"Cozy," I remark, raising an eyebrow. "Are they electric?"

"Yes, though not very modern-looking, I know. But the house belonged to my parents, and my grandparents before that. No one ever got around to updating the fixtures. Besides, these lamps work perfectly fine."

He looks surprised at himself, as if he hadn't meant to let that piece of information slip out.

"I wasn't being facetious. They really are cozy. I like them, Caden. I like the whole rustic ambience of your house."

"Huh." He quickly turns away. Maybe he's not used to humans giving him compliments. Maybe he's just not used to humans, at all—magical or otherwise.

I know better than to inquire further. I shake off my thoughts and follow him.

I called the place *rustic*, but that is an understatement. The low wooden beams overhead, the old-fashioned fittings... the whole thing feels like heading back in time by about a hundred years. For some reason, I find it peaceful. Comforting, almost.

Caden pauses at the end of the corridor.

"You can sleep here," he says, pushing open the door and gesturing.

Hesitantly, I brush past him into the room. He sidles in behind me and lights a small lamp on the bedside table, illuminating a simply furnished bedroom with a braided floor rug beside a wide, rough-hewn bed covered by a colorful blanket. A tall set of wooden drawers sits in the corner. It is neat and clean, but something about the sparsity gives me pause.

"This is your bedroom?"

"Uh huh."

"You spend much time here?"

Caden shrugs. "Not really."

That doesn't surprise me. There's no sign of personality here, or anything bar the necessities.

He huffs. "Do you want to stay in here, or not?"

I tilt my head to one side, eyeing him. Sudden amusement lifts my lips. "Where are *you* going to sleep?"

"I'm a shifter. I don't need to sleep as much as humans do."

Oh, right. I forgot about that. I shuffle my feet, trying to think of ways to prolong the conversation. For some reason, I don't want him to leave just yet.

"You know..." I clasp my hands behind my back, rocking on my heels. "We're going to have to be more convincing in the future. If people are going to buy us as a real couple."

Caden's expression drops into a frown. "What do you mean?"

I circle around the bed and examine a small sculpture on the bedside table—the only décor in the room other than the lamp. It is a detailed wooden carving of a convertible, with a family seated inside—a man at the wheel, a woman in the passenger seat, and a boy with what looks like a large picnic basket beside him, taking up the back seat. All of them have huge and contagious smiles on their faces. Like the colorful blanket on the bed, it's an unexpected thing to find in the otherwise bare, functional space.

Something strange tugs at my heart.

"You can't keep dragging me around like a ragdoll, Caden," I say slowly, stroking my finger over the sculpture before turning to face him. "We're meant to be together. You have to look like..."

He takes a step toward me. His scowl has disappeared and a curious hunger has taken its place. "Like what?"

I swallow thickly, ignoring the pulse of desire that squiggles deep down in my belly. "Like you *want* to touch me."

I pray fervently that he doesn't hear the tremor in my voice. My heart thunders in my ears. I wonder whether Caden's shifter senses allow him to hear it, too.

"Did that kiss a few minutes ago not convince you that I want to touch you?"

The air between us is charged with what feels like electricity.

"Is it enough?" I ask, my voice breathless. "If they expect our scents to be mingled..."

"You're right," he murmurs into the silence. "We should practice some more."

"Just so no-one suspects."

Caden somehow closes the space between us without me even noticing his movement. He lifts a hand and, for a moment, I think he's reaching for my face. But then his fingers slide around my wrist and his thumb presses against my pulse point.

I drop my gaze. No way to disguise my frantic heart rate. No forced sarcasm or fake confidence to hide behind, now.

He guides my hand up to his chest and holds it against his shirt. His chest rises and falls gently beneath my touch, but his heart pounds, at least as fast as my own.

He might look calm, but underneath, he's as agitated as I am.

His eyes haven't left my face. He's watching... waiting for my response.

I curl my fingers into the fabric of his shirt and tug firmly. A slow grin appears, and he steps into my space until he's so close his breath ghosts over my cheek.

His hands bracket my hips on either side, the touch firm and assured, and my body arches into him, almost of its own volition. I shiver as the hardness of his erection grazes my mound.

Goddess, I love the proof of desire—for *me*—that he can't hide, encompassed in that erection.

His thumbs drag over the strip of exposed skin between my shirt top and the waistband of my jeans.

"Feels real," Caden mutters. At least I think that's what he says, but then he shakes his head. I hardly know what he's saying any more, or what I'm saying in return. "I mean, we should definitely make it look real."

His gaze dips to my mouth.

"Yeah." I breathe heavily, my thoughts in a whirl. My body is alive under his touch, and I want...

I want.

Goddess, do I ever want.

My tongue darts out, swiping over my bottom lip. Caden's fingers spasm against my hips, and a groan fills the air.

His groan? Mine? I'm not sure which one of us breaks first. All I know is that one second, we're hovering on the precipice of need, and the next, our mouths surge together in a kiss more frantic than the one we had before.

His essence surrounds me, his enticing scent rising to fill my nostrils. He smells divine. He *tastes* divine. I grind my hips against him, my woman bits molding to his hardness, enjoying the heat and the movement and the pressure between my legs...

I break apart from the kiss, panting hard, trying to find

words. Any words. To stop. To go harder. To leave the room. Or to fuck me until I don't know which way is up.

I don't know what I want.

He lifts me up and dumps me onto the bed—his bed—tumbling on top of me and reclaiming my lips with his.

He pumps against me in a simulation of what I crave, only our clothing stopping the consummation of sex that is only moments away. I clutch at his ass, kneading his flesh and encouraging more. I want him closer. I want him inside me. Now.

This time when we break apart, his breath is as ragged as mine. He stares down into my eyes, crimson flashing deep behind the emerald, and the rush of reality is as effective as a dash of cold water.

Oh, goddess. What are we doing?

The last couple of minutes hits me all at once. I whimper and push at his chest. He shifts away, rolling off me onto his back. I sit up and draw my knees to my chest, wrapping my arms around them to try and settle my system.

Caden sits up too, drawing his legs down over the edge of the bed until he is seated facing away from me. His head drops down and he leans forward, muttering something I don't quite catch.

Several minutes pass, before he stands and turns to face me. "That's enough practice for now, I think."

I nod, not trusting my voice.

He strides across to the door. He pauses there, his head cocked as he stares at me.

"Sleep well, Sophie." His voice is husky. "There's a bathroom next door. It's all yours. There's another downstairs that I'll use. I'll lay out fresh towels if you want to shower in the morning."

He doesn't wait for my reply. I collapse back onto the

pillows with a shaky sigh, feeling the need to pat down my own body and make sure I am all still in one piece.

Holy hell.

How on earth am I ever going to sleep after that?

I lie awake long into the night, thoughts of Caden, and what is coming tomorrow, weighing heavily on my mind.

7

SURPRISINGLY, the quiet surrounds of the farm setting, and the simplicity inherent in the room, lull me into a sleep that is less restless than I expect.

Part of me is afraid to sleep, in case Azriel or one of his demons call me via that half-waking, half-sleeping state that Amethyst traverses when she dream walks. Thankfully, my dreams are relatively normal—albeit filled with images of a sexy hellhound shifter with talented lips and hands, who turns my body into a raging fire of need.

My night might have been demon-free, but my most intimate places are aching and in major need of attention when I wake.

After a quick shower, I conjure up fresh clothing, dressing in a top and jeans, before pulling on my boots and a thick jacket. It is barely light, and so cold that frost still covers the grassy fields around the farm when I step outside. Caden is nowhere in sight, so I assume he must still be asleep in one of the spare bedrooms. In my current need for solitude, his absence suits me just fine. I make my way quietly toward the main road.

I'm not running away, exactly. I just need some time and space to clear my head, before I get stuck into the full charade of being Caden's girlfriend. I didn't expect to find him so attractive, and my own physical reactions are confusing me when the situation is already potentially complicated.

The more I think about Caden's role in this, and his motivation for helping me, the more questions rise up in my mind. Who is he, really, and how did he come to be part of a fallen angel's personal guard? What awful things has he done in service to a bunch of demons? How does Kyan know him, and even more important, why does Kyan trust him? Is Caden truly wanting to get out and stop Azriel once and for all? And if so, why?

It's all well and good for Kyan to say I can trust Caden with my life.

But I'm about to step into the inner circle of an enemy so powerful that no one has been able to stop him so far.

And that's a whole lot of trust to place in someone I've only just met.

Thankfully, once I follow the long and winding track up to the main road, I begin to recognize some of the terrain. I was right yesterday, when we first arrived. Caden's farm isn't far from my own small community town.

The pull of home is strong, and part of me wants to be surrounded by the familiar, at least for a few hours.

Just as I stand there in the road, trying to work out whether to turn back to the farm and wait for Caden to rise, or to try trudging ahead on foot, a rumble sounds behind me. I turn to see a bus crest the hill and continue down toward me. Without thinking, I put out my arm and the bus rolls to a stop.

A short ride later and I'm standing outside my small jewelry store in the middle of town. I'm not sure why I ended up here instead of going directly to my cottage, but I'm guessing that Kyan gave Caden my home address when they made the arrangement for protection.

I need space. For an hour or two, at least. I need to think, without the strange sensations that start up within me every time Caden is near. When I recall what happened last night, a hot flush rises from my chest all the way to the top of my head and then right back down to my clit.

So instead of heading home, I find myself here at the shop, my hair in a messy top knot, my tummy rumbling with hunger, and guilt running through my veins as I wonder what Caden will do when he finds me gone.

Well done, Sapphire. You're really nailing this whole undercover, "fake relationship" thing.

I push open the door and inhale the familiar scent of wood polish and incense, letting it surround and soothe me. It's comforting to know that, no matter what madness is running rampant in the supernatural world, my own little slice of heaven chugs along merrily, the same as it always has, here in the store.

I realize with a dull thud of surprise that it's Saturday morning. I'm supposed to be running a jewelry workshop today, in the small classroom at the rear of the store.

With everything that has been going on, I forgot to cancel the class. At the spa retreat, the daily grind of real life seemed like nothing more than a vague, abstract dream. I was too busy dealing with hellhounds and demons to think about home.

With a pang in my heart, I rush over to the classroom door and wrench it open. I need to set up the room, get out the tools, work out how the lesson will run...

I barrel into the room and skid to a halt.

The room is empty, save for one person. And it's the last person I expect.

"Amethyst!" I clutch at my chest, my heart thudding. "What on earth are you doing here?"

My sister looks up from unstacking chairs off tabletops. She doesn't look surprised to see me. Instead, she waits for me to catch my breath, as cool and composed as ever. Then, she folds her arms.

"Hello, Sapph."

Oh, dear. That tone. It isn't promising.

I venture further into the room, reluctant to meet her gaze. I have a horrible feeling that, if I do, she'll be able to tell exactly what happened last night. Or at least, what *almost* happened, between Caden and me.

"Hey." I fiddle with my hands, then tuck away a loose curl of hair that has fallen out of my bun. "I didn't expect to see you here."

"I'll bet you didn't." Amethyst's shoes clack over the wooden floorboards as she approaches me. She comes to a halt, looking me over. I don't know what she's checking for, but I prickle under the attention. "You left your planner behind. I saw you had a workshop today, so I thought I'd come help you out."

My planner? It seems so long ago that I had the need for a planner. And yet, it has only been a few days since this whole nightmare escalated.

I narrow my eyes at her tone. "You're planning to run my workshop? My *jewelry-making* workshop? Isn't that more Topaz's forte, than yours?"

Topaz has a spell shop back in the city where she also tinkers with gemstones and jewelry, though I suspect she hasn't been back there in a while. Not since she met Kyan and discovered a demon soul collector who works for a fallen angel wants her dead.

Amethyst gives me a wide smile, but the edge remains. "You're welcome."

My eyes dart around the empty room, taking in the half-unstacked tables and chairs. "You don't know the first thing about making jewelry."

"Well," she says, giving an elegant shrug, "I thought I'd mostly let them get on with it. I mean, I could throw in a bonus potion-making lesson, I guess."

My lips twitch. "Of course."

Amethyst has never lost an opportunity to boss people around. And she does love her potions.

She continues to smile at me, with a look that reminds me of a wolf pretending to be a grandma. My suspicions grow.

I know my sister. There's no way she'd come all the way out here to run a jewelry workshop, of all things.

I tilt my head to the side. "Why are you really here?"

"I just told you—"

"Nope. Try again."

Amethyst's eyes narrow. I grin at her, pleased to be on the offensive for a change.

"You did not just drive miles out here for no reason, sis. What is this? Did you plan to run a search for me? And once you found me... what? Keep an eye on me?"

She blanches, and my eyes widen.

"It isn't like that." She takes a step toward me, then seems to think better of it. She clicks her tongue and fiddles with her favorite silver bracelet. "You ran off without a word. I just wanted to make sure you were really okay."

She reaches out and tugs at a loose lock of my hair. "What's going on, Sapph?"

I bat away her hand. "Nothing," I retort. Then I release a sigh. "Actually, something. But it's nothing I can explain easily at the moment."

Amethyst will always be my big sister. Unfortunately, that means that some part of her will always see me as the little girl who trailed around after her and Topaz all those years ago.

Her eyes rake over me. I shift with discomfort. She looks like she's trying to put a puzzle together when she doesn't have all the pieces.

"Sapph...are you *safe?*"

It's an absurd question and we both know it. None of us are *safe*, and we won't be until Azriel, and his demon minions like Luthor, are stopped.

Still, the anxiety that underlies her words is genuine.

"Yes, I am. I have a..." I don't even know what to call Caden. In the end, I settle for, "Friend. A hellhound friend of Kyan's, and he's helping me out. Keeping an eye on things and offering a bit of protection. I'm not alone, Ammie."

Some of the tension drains out of her face.

"Okay. What's his name?"

"Caden. Different shifter pack to Kyan and Dane, but Kyan trusts him. And so do I."

As I say the words out loud, I realize it's true. I do trust Caden. I have no idea *how* I know he's trustworthy, other than my usual magical ability to discern things that are nebulous and unclear, but in my heart, I know I can trust him to have my back.

The knowledge lifts a weight off my shoulders and I straighten, not even realizing till this very second how heavy and bowed I was due to stress.

I'm not alone anymore. At least, I won't be alone, till this current situation is resolved.

I want nothing more than to tell Ammie everything. About Caden, and about last night. About going undercover with a member of Azriel's guard, and how I'm beginning to worry that I've bitten off more than I can chew. I want her to fix everything, just like she used to.

She takes a step forward and folds me into her arms. I

sink into her embrace, enjoying it before squeezing tight and letting go.

Time to stand up without Ammie and Topaz propping me up.

With a heavy heart, I turn away so she doesn't see the tears glistening in my eyes.

"I'll be fine, sis," I say. "I've got it under control. And Caden is there to help. Enjoy teaching my class!"

Just before I walk out of the classroom, leaving her standing alone, I turn and study her. The look in her eyes as she returns my stare is one of fear, and pride.

I carry that look with me all the way home to my cottage.

I climb up the porch steps and touch my hand to the lock like I'm in a dream.

Beneath my familiar touch, the door lock releases. I've only been gone a couple of weeks altogether, but as I push open the door, it feels more like years. Long shadows stretch over the floor, and the lowered blinds cast a darkness over the place. I'm not afraid of the darkness; my power stems from the shadows, after all. But today, it is like walking into a stranger's place rather than arriving home.

I wander over to the long mirror in the hallway and stare at myself. I look exactly the same as I always do. Maybe slightly more disheveled than usual, but there is nothing in the reflection that indicates any of the momentous things I've been through in the past days and weeks.

Even though I had a shower at Caden's, I feel like I need another. Too much to deal with, and I know the hard part is only just beginning. After I step out of the welcome steam and wrap myself tightly in my soft robe, I feel marginally better.

I text Caden, letting him know where I am, feeling guilty as I know he will have discovered my absence by now. I imagine a mix of annoyance and worry. Hopefully, my text alleviates his concern.

After a few minutes, my phone buzzes.

No problem, honey. I will see you later xx

Honey? My teeth clench, then laughter wins, bubbling up and out. I'm still grinning while I heat up a bowl of oatmeal porridge in the microwave. Afterward, I slump down on the sofa in my comfiest sweatpants, and my eyelids begin to flutter closed. I know Caden will be by to collect me, but for now, my senses are lulled by the familiarity of my own place, after weeks spent drifting around the countryside, running between battles and ambushes and everything in between.

I relax into the sofa cushions, and before I know it, I'm fast asleep.

A buzzing sound jolts me awake. I leap up off the sofa, casting wildly around for intruders. I'm disoriented in the darkness of the room. It takes a second to get my bearings, and to remember that I'm back home and in my own living room.

The buzzing starts up again and my eyes snap to the coffee table. My phone is lit up, and Caden's name is on the display. I also notice it is past seven p.m. already. I must have slept away most of the day.

I scramble to pick up the phone and hold it to my ear. "Caden? What is it?"

"Hello Sophie."

My heart races, and I tell myself it is because I just got woken up unexpectedly. It can't be because his voice makes me think of decadent rivers of melted chocolate dripping down my body.

No, couldn't be that, at all.

"I'm calling about Azriel." Caden's tone is determinedly neutral. Right. Someone must be monitoring our conversation.

"What about him, honey?" I ask, equally carefully.

Amusement laces his next words. "He's heard about my new girlfriend. He wants to meet you. Honey."

Every muscle in my body locks up.

"What?" I choke out. "When?"

"Tonight, Sophie. Right now, in fact. Get dressed. I'll be there to pick you up in an hour."

8

I DROP the phone onto the couch, my heart hammering. I take a couple of deep, calming breaths, trying to stop the rush of panic that threatens to overtake me.

"Just remember," I mumble out loud, "you are Sophie. An ordinary human woman who knows next to nothing about the supernatural world. You'll be there with your big, strong boyfriend, and you have nothing to be afraid of."

I catch a glimpse of myself in the mirror and hold my chin high, stretching my mouth into a smile. The woman in the mirror smiles back, tightness around the eyes evident, but maybe, just maybe...

"I can pull this off."

I say it again, just for good measure. *I can do this*. It is what I wanted, after all. A chance to get close to Azriel and look for a chink in his seemingly impenetrable armor. That chance might have come sooner than expected, and in a most unusual way, but that doesn't mean I'm not going to act on it, when a gift horse has just been offered up.

I spend the next fifteen minutes or so pulling out every item of clothing in my wardrobe and laying them across the bed. I hold up garment after garment, before tossing them aside with renewed frustration.

What does one wear to a gathering of creatures from the Other-world? When you are invited to meet your boyfriend's boss—and he happens to be an evil fallen angel?

Caden hasn't given me any pointers in relation the dress code. I don't want to turn up overdressed, but if I wear jeans and boots, I'll stick out if everyone is in formal gear.

In the end, I opt for a simple black slip dress and small heels, with a casual jacket that I can don if everyone else is not formal. The dress was a present from Topaz a couple of years ago and it always gives me confidence when I wear it. I can do with the confidence boost at this moment. I smooth down the satiny fabric with my fingers and then reach up to my hair, toying with it, before deciding to leave it loose around my shoulders.

I keep my makeup relatively simple and light. On a last-minute whim, I reach for my dark red lipstick, then re-examine myself in the mirror. This time, the reflection that stares back is more self-assured.

My buzzer sounds, and the trepidation returns. I scoop up my purse and hurry to the intercom, pressing the button to speak. "I'll be right down."

There's no response. I didn't expect any. Caden doesn't seem to speak unless he has to.

My heart is in my mouth as I descend the narrow staircase. It's only when I reach the bottom, that it suddenly occurs to me that Caden might have brought the motorbike.

Oh, goddess. There's no way I can ride a bike in this dress!

My mind is still racing when I pull open the door and let myself out into the night. It's not cold, but a shiver runs through me nonetheless as I catch sight of a vehicle, with a familiar dark-clad figure inside.

Familiar, and yet, not. This time, Caden is in a charcoal-colored suit, with a black shirt and tie giving him the look of a sexy mafia boss.

I can't tell whether it is my ever-present fear about what I'm about to face, or something altogether more pleasurable, that causes my insides to clench when I stare at him.

One thing is certain. There's no turning back now.

At least he didn't bring the motorcycle this time. My pulse rate picks up when he opens the passenger side door, gesturing for me to climb inside.

I slink past him, self-conscious about my skimpy attire. Is it suitable? Is there too much on show? The damn man hasn't taken his assessing gaze off me since the moment I stepped out the door.

I settle against the butter-soft leather upholstery and surreptitiously adjust the neckline of my dress, hiking it as high as I can. Maybe I can pretend that handsome men pick me up in luxury cars like this all the time. Might make the vulnerability spearing through my system slightly more bearable.

"Where are we going?" The question slips past my lips as he turns the key in the ignition.

"Not far."

Before he pulls out, he leans over and brushes his lips over my hair. I can't help the shiver at our connection, though his words, almost non-existent against my ear, are equally as effective in creating tension.

"Eyes and ears are everywhere."

I give him a surreptitious nod, and his features relax a notch.

When we take off, silence fills the vehicle. I don't know how to address the topic of my sudden flight from his place this morning, especially if others might be listening in.

"I just needed to check on a few things at home," I say,

deciding against the truth. *I needed space. I don't understand anything about this. About us.*

"All good," he says noncommittally, and I settle back, unsure who might be listening and what I'm allowed to say.

He handles the car with an expert precision, traveling much faster than I'm used to. The streets around us blur into a haze of neon light; soon enough, we leave town altogether, and there's nothing beyond the headlights but a long, snaking road stretching out into the darkness.

"What should I expect?" I ask, when I can't bear the silence for a second longer.

His gaze flicks toward me. "The unexpected."

Annoyance pulses through me. "An enigmatic man might be sexy, on paper, but in reality... it's not helpful."

"Forgive me. I didn't intend..." Caden trails off. "Sexy? Only on paper?"

"Never mind." I press my lips together, wishing I didn't have a habit of blurting out whatever is in my head. Then I remember the potential listeners and shoot him what I hope is a seductive glance. "I can show you later what I think in-person sexy should look like. If you want?"

His fingers convulse on the steering wheel; it's a strangely human gesture, coming from him. "I do want that, Sophie. Very much."

His tone is husky and doesn't sound fake, at all.

I swallow hard, wondering if he will hold me to it—and whether I want him to hold me to it.

Then I remember where we're headed, and any desire that might be simmering between us fades away.

I want to ask if he thinks Azriel will recognize me from the battlefield. I mean, I *was* on the beach in that battle against the demons, and again at the resort. I faced Azriel himself, together with Ammie and Tee, though I think his focus was mainly on Ammie who had called him forth via her dream walking.

Probably something I should have considered earlier, I guess. But I've been so focused on wanting to do *something*, that the smaller details slipped my mind, till now.

Self-doubt must cloud my expression, because Caden removes a hand from the wheel and lays it on my thigh. He squeezes my flesh, then releases me, but not before the warmth from his fingertips heats my blood in a way that both calms, and excites.

"Azriel is a celestial being," he says, and I hear the warning beneath his bland explanation. "His power is unlike any other creature in this, or any, universe."

I nod, trying to swallow down my growing fear. "He sounds... unique."

Caden's mouth tightens. "He is."

My gaze turns to the blackness outside. It mirrors the emptiness spiraling through my chest, turning it hollow, as I contemplate the task that lies ahead.

We spend the rest of the journey in silence, each lost in our own thoughts.

———

THE CAR SLOWS as the road narrows. We turn off onto a small, winding lane. Trees form a natural archway overhead, their bare, spindly limbs stretching down from the darkness above. The terrain seems suitably barren—does this area remind Azriel of the Otherworld? Is the black crystal cave that Amethyst described from her dream walking situated somewhere near here? Perhaps on this very land?

I don't know what the Otherworld is like, but I imagine it full of darkness and shadow, all burnt and ashy and smoke-filled, from flames that never switch off. Every so often, when Caden moves unexpectedly, a whiff of smoke rises into my nostrils. It is not unpleasant, but it is still a reminder of his origins.

I suspect the memories he has from his childhood are nothing at all like mine.

Was it a place where nothing had the choice to grow or thrive? One day, if I get the chance, I will ask Caden more about where he grew up and what it was like. Maybe I have it all wrong.

I peer out the car window, looking for any signs of habitation. Is this Azriel's permanent lair in the human realm, or does he simply occupy one place and then another, depending on whim?

The road beneath the car's wheels becomes gravelly and uneven. In the dim light I make out half-bare undergrowth on both sides of us; tall hedgerows that seem at first sight twisted and misshapen from neglect, and then, when I blink a couple of times, they are neat and welcoming and full of life.

Which is the truth?

From time to time, my eyes catch small flickers of movement. Things dart in amongst the foliage, too fast for me to get a good look.

Rabbits, I hope. I shudder to think of what else might lurk in the shadows surrounding a fallen angel's earthly home.

Soon enough, the road widens. Tall, elaborate gates loom ahead of us. Light glows from lanterns hanging on carved stone pillars either side of the entrance.

The gates open for the car, seemingly without anyone operating them. Caden drives through without even slowing. A glance at his face tells me nothing; if he's nervous at all, he doesn't show it. He looks almost bored as he pulls up in front of a huge house.

The whole setting looks like something out of a horror movie, beautiful but with dark secrets waiting to break free, and I have to struggle not to burst into nervous giggles.

"Wait here," he mutters, and slides out of the vehicle.

His trudging footsteps fade into the night. I force myself to relax. I can't help but wonder if I've been caught in an elaborate trap. Was I wrong to trust Caden?

Is this truly a horror movie, where the too-stupid-to-live heroine is about to meet her grisly end?

I'm tempted to call on my magic. Reach out, just a tentacle or two, to get a sense of what might be about to happen. But if this is Azriel's territory, then using magic is a big no-no, especially if he's expecting Sophie the non-magical human woman to accompany Caden inside.

Before I have the chance to consider further, the car door opens, and Caden stands there with his hand extended.

"Let's go, Sophie."

The name is a reminder that we are not alone, and I shoot him a wide smile that hopefully hides my underlying terror.

"Thanks, babe." I place my hand in his and climb out, breathing in the cool night air.

"No problem. Babe." He returns my smile with a bland grin, but squeezes my fingers, now interlaced with his, in a mute show of support.

Into the lair of the monster we go.

Tiny goosebumps rise up on my arms as Caden pulls me in close beside him and guides me toward the house.

Well, house is hardly an appropriate term for the enormous mansion before us.

It is huge and imposing, several levels high, with innumerable windows and a wide set of stairs leading up to the vast front door that is flanked on either side by Greek-style columns.

Caden guides me up the steps to the portico. The pressure of our joined hands is the only thing anchoring me to earth. I hold my focus on his touch as we climb to the top and reach the massive set of double doors.

Just like the gates, the doors open automatically the second we set foot on the top step. Someone is waiting for us on the other side: a tall and strikingly attractive woman with a long, glossy black braid that snakes down over a bare shoulder, her strapless black velvet dress revealing flawless alabaster skin, and a set of brilliant green eyes that rake Caden before turning to study me.

She has high, arched eyebrows and sharply delineated features, and she would be beautiful were it not for the sudden flare of crimson in her eyes when she lifts her nose as if to scent me. Her gaze swivels from me to Caden and back again and her mouth thins. Then she blinks.

The crimson disappears and a fake smile widens her lips.

Great. Another hellhound. Who looks better in a black dress than I do, and most assuredly is not happy to see me hanging off Caden's arm.

She taps her fingers against the door frame with obvious impatience. Her fingernails are black, long, and elegantly tapered. I resist the urge to check the state of my own, knowing that recent events have left them stumpy and broken from chewing on them.

If I were anywhere else but here, I would push a tiny burst of energy into my fingertips, creating perfectly French-manicured tips that would give this woman a run for her money.

She turns away as if I'm not worth looking at any longer, before striding off into the cavernous space with an exaggerated swish of her hips. She doesn't look back.

We—or at least, I—have been catalogued and dismissed, just like that.

I straighten my dress, which doesn't need straightening, and glance at Caden, who gestures grandly. *You first.*

Here goes nothing.

I take a deep breath and step over the threshold.

9

THE FOYER ENTRANCE is as huge and opulent as the exterior led me to expect. I have to crane my neck to take in the high ceiling, the elaborately molded columns, and the shimmering gilt on huge floor-to-ceiling mirrors that extend the entryway in an optical illusion of even more grandeur.

Candles glow softly from every alcove, and black marble tiles flecked with silver gleam beneath my feet.

Ammie told me about the crystal cave where she met with Azriel. It seems the angel has upgraded, but obviously he still likes his décor black and sparkly.

"Come." The voice in my ear startles me out of my reverie. I look up at Caden. He releases my fingers and cups his hand around my elbow, leading me further inside. "He's waiting for you."

My feet seem to have a mind of their own; they propel me forward while my mind skitters all over the place. My skin prickles with the knowledge that, somewhere within these walls, Azriel is lying in wait.

I catch sight of Caden's face in every mirror we pass—why are there so many mirrors? His features are set in a stony expression. My reflected face, on the other hand, is pale and my eyes stormy. I have to figure out how to contain my emotions, but with every step we take, dread grows.

This was a ridiculous mistake. What was I thinking, to step into his lair like this? I've made it super-easy for Azriel to strike down at least one of our witchy trio. And with me gone, he will find it far easier to get to Ammie and Tee.

Have I condemned us all to a dreadful death—or *worse*, for Tee, if they take her soul into servitude?

My "knowing" magic has led me here. The belief that I need to get close to Azriel in order to end this, once and for all. But what if my powers steered me wrong? What if I've misinterpreted the flashes of knowing, and "ending this" means death for *us*, rather than the fallen angel?

I swallow hard as nausea flares in my belly.

What have I done?

Caden, too, seems to display a growing reluctance. He slows his walk to snail pace, as if he's wading against a strong tide. Like some inner force is pushing him back.

"You sure?" he murmurs.

"Mm hmm. Yep." *No. Not at all.*

When we finally come to a standstill at the edge of a vast, gilded set of doors, he turns to face me.

"What is it?" I ask, when he doesn't say anything.

His eyes scan my face.

"Please be careful," he whispers, but before he can say more, the door before us creaks open.

The man who stands there is tall and broad, with pale skin and dark hair, and he is wearing some kind of swirling robe. He gives us an easy smile that doesn't meet his eyes. The sight of those eyes—dark pools empty of life—sends a chill through my blood.

Not a man. *Demon.*

The word rustles through my mind. My feet are rooted to the spot, and my uneasy smile freezes on my lips.

"He will see you now." The demon doesn't spare a glance for Caden. His croaky voice is directed at me.

Caden's grip tightens around my elbow. He makes to step forward, before his way is blocked by someone thrusting out a large hand.

"Only the girl."

I shoot a panicked look at Caden, whose mouth curls downward. His eyes flash in the first real sign of emotion since we arrived.

"No," he says bluntly.

"The Master wishes to see her... alone."

"I would prefer not to leave her unaccompanied," Caden says. The tension in his voice is hard to miss. "She is unfamiliar with our ways."

The creature shakes his head. "The Master said the girl only."

There is clearly no arguing. The demon won't let Caden through. But the knowledge inside me swells.

I need to be here. This is the correct path.

I should back my own magical powers—my *knowing*—that tell me I need to be here.

One way or another, I *know* I have to do this.

I take a deep breath and catch Caden's eye. "It's okay. I'll be fine."

Caden's eyes narrow. A storm of emotion swirls in their green depths, and I glimpse the crimson hovering beneath. "Sophie..."

The name is a warning; a reminder that I am human and non-magical, and merely Caden's new girlfriend, meeting his boss.

I nod and give him a grin that tries to hide my skittering nerves.

"I'll be fine," I repeat, and I pat the fingers still clutching my elbow, before detaching from his grip. "I promise I won't say anything to embarrass you, hun."

His eyes bore into mine.

"I'll be waiting," he murmurs eventually. I know in my bones that he won't leave this place without me. He will come running if he senses I'm in trouble.

The demon steps back and beckons me forward. I follow him inside.

With a soft, final *click*, the door shuts behind us, locking Caden out.

I FIND myself in a dimly lit study.

Full bookshelves line the walls, and a tall-backed leather chair rests behind a large desk. A lamp softly illuminates the space, glinting off the elegant inkwell, the brass handles on the cabinet behind the desk, and a small globe of the earth positioned at one corner of the desk.

Is this where he makes his plans for world domination?

The space is tranquil. Peaceful, even.

It's also completely empty.

I whirl, searching for the demon who let me in. He's nowhere to be seen.

Unsettled, I rush back to where I entered and try the handle of the door. It is locked.

I take a deep breath and square my shoulders, certain I'm being watched. I am now literally in the lair of the monster.

Don't let them know you're afraid.

I stroll across the room, trailing my fingertips across the books, like there is nowhere else I'd rather be right now. I come to a halt in front of the window.

My eyes widen and I suck in a breath. I wasn't expecting that view.

The dark shapes of trees surround a vast, glimmering lake whose surface is as black as pitch.

Is the black crystal cave out there somewhere in the shadows, beside the equally mysterious lake?

My magic stirs involuntarily, drawn to the beautiful darkness, and I have to focus hard to tamp the curl of power back down. This is the last place I should release any hint of my magical energy.

But... it's so *beautiful*... that darkness. It must hold so much *power*...

"A delightful view, is it not?"

The voice comes out of nowhere and I jump. A rush of cool breath caresses my bare shoulder. I turn, taking a quick step back from the tall being crowding me.

He looks both human-like, and otherworldly.

Azriel.

He has shoulder-length dark hair and human clothing—a dark suit similar to Caden's, in fact. His hands are tucked neatly behind him, and he isn't looking directly at me, but rather, staring over my shoulder at the view outside. His expression is calm, almost serene.

But his skin is so pale it is almost translucent, and despite the human-like features, his eyes are black in the middle and glowing silver around the edges where the whites would normally be.

A wave of terror washes over me, followed by the realization that he has likely been here in the room with me from the moment I arrived. The demon at the door, who let me in to this study, likely wasn't a demon after all. It must have been...

You. I almost blurt out the word, only just managing to swallow it back in time.

"Hello, sir." My eyes are wide, and I feign uncertainty as I consider what an innocent human woman would think and how she might react in this situation. For sure, she'd be nervous, at the very least... "It is a lovely view. Pleased to meet you. I'm—"

"Sapphire Redferne." His gaze lands directly on me at last and I have to fight to remain upright. My knees tremble as if I've just run a marathon and am about to collapse.

Bam. Too-stupid-to-live just got real.

Azriel smiles pleasantly, as if he hasn't just sucked all the air out of my lungs with his pronouncement.

I clear my throat, a lump of emotion rendering me speechless. I consider calling on that black pool of darkness outside, drawing all my magic up and trying to blast him into ash. Or at least, back to the Otherworld, and then slam the etheric rifts shut so he can't get back here again.

But I already know I would never get the chance.

I can *feel* his power, surrounding me, caressing my skin with a fingerless touch that makes my nerves screech. Amethyst said she could barely breathe in his presence, the first time she dream walked and met him. Even now, when I suspect he has most of his celestial power tamped down, I know I am no match for Azriel when it comes to magical ability.

Not without Ammie and Topaz by my side.

Azriel continues to stare at me with that same calm expression. He doesn't seem angry. Perhaps curious. Like he's enjoying a game and waiting to see what I'll do before he decides his next move.

Don't freak out. If he wanted to kill you immediately, you would already be dead.

That isn't a very reassuring thought.

I meet his unearthly gaze with some difficulty.

You have magic, I remind myself. *Magic that likes the darkness in which he cloaks himself. You are not defenseless. Not by a long shot.*

"How did you know?" I try to emulate his calm attitude, though inside, my heart pumps doubly hard. *Maybe I was wrong. Maybe he did notice me on that battlefield at the resort.*

"I didn't know, until just then, when you turned and looked at me." He tilts his head, studying me. "Your resemblance to your sister is uncanny."

His eyes flare and I can't help taking another tiny step back. My back is right against the window, now.

"And your cousin. I see the lovely Topaz in you, too. Now that I'm looking. You all share the same... blood, after all."

"Of course." I reach back and grip the edge of the window ledge, focusing on the feel of something solid and grounding. "You met Amethyst, I believe."

Damn. Shut up. No need to remind him that we tried to kill him, last time we saw him.

It is becoming increasingly difficult to breathe. I feel lightheaded, as if I'm about to faint, and I suck in a slow, deep breath and sidle away. His mouth quirks into a smile, as if he notices my discomfort and takes joy from it.

"That is certainly one way of putting it." Azriel takes a step closer. "In fact, you are the only Redferne witch I have not had the pleasure of meeting up close and personal."

My memory floods with images from that night. I was there with Ammie and Tee, of course, but the fallen angel's attention was elsewhere. It was what I had been counting on, but I didn't factor in my resemblance to Ammie and Topaz.

I force my features to remain neutral while I stare into the eyes of the one responsible for all the death and destruction and terror that has dogged our lives for so long.

Play along. Don't get angry—stay meek and answer his questions. He's the one in control. For now.

"Sapphire. You are the youngest of your family, correct?"

"Yes."

"What made you decide to come here, to my earthly home?"

"I wanted to meet you for myself." Something deep inside prompts me to add honestly, "There is a darkness in my magic, that I don't fully understand. It... drew me here. To you."

Azriel raises a brow, but a gleam of interest in those dead eyes whispers to life. "Some might call you foolhardy."

I shrug. The casual gesture feels out of place here, in this elaborate study, in the presence of a celestial, even though a fallen one. One of the spaghetti straps of my dress threatens to slip down, and I fix it back in place.

"My sister would agree with you," I say. "And my cousin. I guess you do have something in common with them, after all."

Azriel lets out a laugh, unexpected and low. It reverberates off the walls and high ceiling, filling the space and sending spikes directly into my soul.

The eerie sound does not inspire me to laugh alongside of him.

"Tell me, Sapphire." The humor leaves his features as quickly as it arrived, but the effect remains, sizzling in my blood. He glides forward, the movement fluid and graceful, closing the space between us. "Are you afraid of me?"

I pause, weighing my answer before responding. *He already knows I'm terrified. He can sense it.* I go with more honesty. "Yes. I am. Very much."

He tilts his chin, regarding me closely. "Why?"

My tongue darts out to dampen my suddenly dry lips. *You're a fallen and you command an army of demons and evil hell-hounds.* "You want to hurt my family."

He nods, like the answer is expected. I have the uncomfortable feeling I'm being examined, like an insect under a magnifying glass. What does he see? Do I pass muster?

"And yet," he muses, "you are still drawn here, to my darkness."

"Yes."

"Interesting." He circles me, gliding all the way around me and back to the front. "Would you believe me, Sapphire, if I said all I wanted was peace?"

I look into his dark yet glowing eyes, taking in the silky-smooth cadence of his voice that washes over me like a calming balm. I fight it off, wondering if he is trying to seduce me. Not physically, but magically.

Do I believe him? *Yes. No. I don't know.*

My power surges inside me, a reminder of who I am. My thoughts coalesce into clarity. I don't believe him.

Not in a million fucking years.

"How is peace possible?" I whisper, pretending submission to his will.

"Your cousin was marked for death."

Despite myself, I lean closer, trying to catch every word.

"The Fae saved her by dipping in to the old magic. The oldest kind. In doing so, they interfered with fate. No one can change the balance of the cosmos, Sapphire, without expecting a consequence for that action. The Fae may have caused the ripple in the ether, but it was your cousin who initiated things. That was very naughty of her, was it not?"

I shake my head to try and clear the strange, muddled sensation that slips over me every time he speaks. The tone of his voice is hypnotic. It would be so easy to believe him...

"Then your sister called out to me," he continues. "With her dream walking. She summoned me against my will with the intention of destroying me, along with my followers. I merely defended myself. Protected my friends. Would you not have done the same?"

"I..." I blink in confusion. It does sound... very reasonable, when he puts it like that.

His eyes are intent upon mine.

"I hadn't thought of it that way," I admit.

He steps forward, herding me backward, until the backs of my legs press against the edge of the desk. He looms over me, the towering form blocking out the warm light around us. I struggle to retain my focus.

He's trying to take me apart mentally, piece by piece, and remake me in his mold.

One of his long, pale fingers loops around a lock of my hair and tugs gently.

"You are very lovely, my dear."

I'm stronger than he realizes. I have to be.

"Th... thank you." With effort, I manage to push back the encroaching confusion. I conjure a mental shield, even while swaying closer toward him.

The push-pull of his angelic allure is giving me a headache.

"Serve me, Sapphire," he murmurs. "I would be honored to have you join my ranks. Think of it. You and your hell-hound Caden can serve together, side by side."

The mention of Caden causes something warm to kindle inside my chest. An ember of something I can't quite name. In my desperate struggle to remain outside Azriel's influence, I label the warm feeling... *hope.*

The faint resistance gives me the strength I need to make a decision. I pray to the goddess it is not the wrong one, for all of us.

I flutter my eyelashes, trying to give the impression of bemusement.

"I don't seem able to... think..." I push my brows into a faint frown, as if I don't understand what is going on. "Yes, all right. I will join you."

My frown clears.

Azriel smiles, though his eyes remain cold and intent as they bore into mine. Does he really believe he has won me over that easily?

"Excellent." He reaches out a pale finger and strokes the very tip down the side of my face. It takes everything in me not to flinch away. Not to shudder. Not to bring up the contents of my roiling stomach all over his pristine floor.

"You have pleased me, child."

Before I can think up an appropriate response, his hand slides lower, down to my throat.

His fingers lock around my neck. There is no way he can avoid being aware of the frantic thump of my heartbeat.

I don't dare to move; every muscle in my body stiffens.

"Never forget." He leans close, his breath whispering like a deadly caress into my ear.

I clench my fingers together to contain the tremble of terror.

"One word from me will silence your beloved sister forever," he says. "Your cousin, too. Not to mention that hellhound you hold so dear. You are mine, now, Sapphire. Mine."

Caden

THE DOOR to Azriel's inner sanctum remains closed for what feels like an eternity.

The carved wooden surface, elaborately gilded with a mix of silver and gold trim, glimmers mockingly at me in the low light of the hallway. I can't hear any noise beyond the door, but I can't take my eyes off it, either.

I glare at the entrance as I lean against the opposite wall, hating the feeling of helplessness. Hating that I now have someone else I need to worry about, beyond Patrick and one or two others of the pack who also want out. Sapphire is courageous enough—and stupid enough—to put herself directly in harm's way and now I am responsible for her safety, too.

Not that I can do a thing to save her, if Azriel decides he wants to destroy her during this meeting. Part of me wants to punch and kick my way in, and then whisk her out of his presence. Consequences be damned. But that would be one of the dumbest moves I've ever made—and I've made some pretty dumb moves in my life so far.

I hate this place. Every facet of the exterior, and every piece of the elegant, opulent interior is fraudulent—designed to impress and lure visitors inside. Seduce them with wealth and luxury and promises of whatever it is Azriel deems they desire, until it's too late to turn back from the path that leads into eternal darkness.

I would burn the whole place to the ground if I could guarantee that Azriel wouldn't rise from the ashes, even stronger and more evil than before. But I can't. The power wielded by him is celestial. It might be tainted and warped, but it is still a force far greater than one hellhound shifter— or even a whole pack of hellhound shifters—can defeat.

The fact that Sapphire is here, now, in the heart of Azriel's web of lies, possibly being lured in to do his bidding, makes my blood surge with fear for her wellbeing.

My hands curl into fists at my sides.

I am useless out here. He could destroy her in an instant, merely with the crook of his little finger. I am a man of action and I need to be by Sapphire's side, on the other side of that closed door. Where I belong.

Protecting the witch as I have been tasked by Kyan.

At long, long last, the lock clicks once more, and the door swings open with a low *creak.*

Azriel stands in the doorway.

He's in his most common human form now—his favorite when he has any dealings with the mortals of this world. He looks like a man, tall and imposing, with dark hair and a narrow, pale face. I don't know if he could ever be called handsome, given the blackness of his eyes that glimmer with a non-mortal glow no matter what form he takes.

A slow smile plays about the corners of his mouth as he meets my gaze. He seems pleased about something.

He shifts slightly to one side and my gaze drifts, landing on Sapphire standing beside him. His arm is draped over her shoulders. A snarl rises up from my shifter at the lack of distance between their bodies.

Then I notice her pallor. She is almost as pale as he is, and she stares at me wide-eyed, as if she's seen a ghost.

A spike of alarm jolts through me. *Has he done something to her mind? Her body?*

I stare hard at Sapphire, trying not to give anything away to Azriel. But I *need* to know if she's okay. My shifter needs to know, or it will never settle down inside of me.

Then, just as I begin to despair about her sanity, one of her eyelids drops in a tiny, almost imperceptible half-wink.

I force myself not to allow any emotion to show in my face, given Azriel's attention is currently firmly on me. *I am stone. I am hewn from stone. Show nothing.*

Relief, mixed with a tinge of anger at this whole situation, flickers in my chest but I keep it contained. That half-wink from Sapphire is as much reassurance as I'll get. But it is enough. It has to be—for now.

"We will have words later, Caden, about why you mentioned to your pack that your new girlfriend's name is Sophie, and not by her true name, Sapphire Redferne."

Forget being hewn from stone. My mouth drops open and I stare at Azriel.

He... *knows?* And she's still alive? And seemingly unhurt?

How is that possible?

My gaze slides to Sapphire, to the slightly unfocused look in her eyes and the almost vacuous smile gracing her lips.

Realization dawns. He thinks he has her. But that tiny wink said otherwise. She was alone with him in his lair, for all that time, and somehow, she is still in possession of her faculties.

Respect for her inner strength flares.

I can number on one hand the people who have resisted the lure of this particular fallen angel's offerings.

"For now, you will both join me for dinner." Azriel steps out of the room, using his grip on Sapphire's shoulders to force her to move in sync with him. The door to the inner sanctum slams shut behind them.

My stomach twists as his arms drops down to rest casually around her waist.

"I trust that will be acceptable to you?" he says, one eyebrow rising.

I give him a stiff nod.

"Of course," I manage, though my voice is slightly rough around the edges. I'm hoping he'll chalk up my odd behavior to nerves about the name thing. Does he realize she is not actually my girlfriend?

I study his firm hold on her. No, I'm sure he hasn't realized that. He is keeping hold of her because he wants to push me over the edge into jealousy. Damned if he isn't doing a good job of it already.

She's not *your girlfriend.* Why I even have to remind myself of that is beyond me. But if he thinks we are in a relationship, then he'll expect at least some show of annoyance from me at his hands all over her. Maybe I don't have to remain quite so hewn from stone as I first thought.

I allow a low growl to rumble up out of my throat, and Azriel's mouth twitches up.

My fists clench. I was correct. He wants to stir up trouble between me and Sapphire.

The urge to jump across the hallway and tear out his throat rises up, but I stuff it back down. There is no way I would ever get to him before he would smite me down. Otherwise, I'd have attempted an attack a thousand times over already.

He would destroy me in an instant, and then take an eternity to torture her as penance for daring to be my girlfriend.

Get it together, man. This is what you signed up for.

With my feet dragging like leaden weights, I have no choice but to follow Azriel and Sapphire down the corridor.

Like a tame puppy.

WE END UP IN A LONG, high-ceilinged dining room. Azriel doesn't do more than glance at the three servant underlings in attendance, and yet, by the time we are seated at the grand table, two extra places have already been set. I stare at the collection of polished silverware, the cut-crystal wine decanter in front of Azriel's place, and the roses that make up the floral centerpiece. The petals are a dark, dusky red, the color of spilled blood.

The color of Sapphire's lipstick-covered lips.

The paleness of her complexion makes her beautiful mouth stand out, and I can't keep my eyes off her as she smiles at Azriel and leans close to allow him to murmur something into her ear. His hand on her bare arm makes my skin crawl and sets my teeth on edge.

Can he see how close I am to shifting? Can he read the crimson tinge of the hellhound in my eyes, and if so, does he want to taunt me beyond reason into madness?

Fallen angel or not, Azriel will be playing with fire if he pushes me too far beyond my limits.

I don't dare to make eye contact with Sapphire for more than a handful of seconds at a time. We're still being watched closely; Azriel is all smiles as he raises his glass in a toast, but I read the truth in his soulless gaze. He is waiting for one of us to slip up—expecting it.

Keep your enemies close.

Is that what we're doing?

Or is it what *he* is doing, right now, while he toys with us?

I barely taste any of the food placed in front of me. I eat mechanically, over several courses, speaking only when spoken to, and when dinner is over, I cannot even say what it was I've just eaten.

Eventually, the excruciating ordeal comes to an end, and Azriel bids us farewell with a show of regret as fake as everything else about him.

"I have many things to attend to," he says, waving forward a servant—one of his demons. "And I am sure the two of you —such a dear, dear couple—have much to discuss. We will meet again. Soon, Sapphire Redferne."

He steps back into the shadows around the edges of the room and, between one blink of my eyelids and the next, disappears. I am used to the ways of the Otherworld, but Sapphire's mouth drops open and she blinks as if in shock at his dramatic exit.

Then she shakes her head in a rueful manner and transfers her attention to the demon now holding open the door. She takes a deep breath, as if breaking free of a trance, and lifts her head as she strides past and out onto the terraced entry area.

I follow quickly, noting that we have been caught up in Azriel's lair for most of the night. The first pale fingers of dawn have begun to creep over the horizon, and the air is crisp and cool outside.

I raise my nose and breathe deeply, needing the freshness to wash away the sour taste in my mouth.

The taste of bitterness. Bitterness at being so helpless, so vulnerable.

Bitterness at the lack of choice about what I want for my future. For my pack's future.

We will never be free while Azriel walks the earth.

Sapphire starts to speak as soon as we reach the bottom of the stairs, but I slide an arm around her waist and pull her close as we move onto the gravel driveway.

"Not here," I murmur, brushing my lips across the top of her hair for good measure.

Just to keep up appearances.

"Holy goddess," she breathes. "That was…"

"Yes." I want to know everything that transpired between her and Azriel, but I'll have to wait a little longer to satisfy my curiosity.

I drop off the car in one of Patrick's garage outbuildings. It'll get dismantled for parts by the end of the week. It's the safest option; Azriel could have done anything to it while we were at the mansion.

Sapphire looks askance at me as I urge her into a beat-up old truck that I stashed in Patrick's garage the day before. I explain the precaution as we hit the main road.

"Finally." She exhales heavily, slumping back against the seat. "So, we're safe to talk, now?"

"As we'll ever be," I mutter darkly. My hands flex against the steering wheel as I glance over at her. Aside from the dark, almost bruise-like circles under her eyes, she seems unhurt. "Are you all right?"

"I'm fine." She tucks a strand of hair behind her ear and gives me a shaky smile. "I think."

"What happened when you were alone with him?" It's a struggle to keep my voice calm. I want to pull the truck over and demand every detail from her. I suspect that wouldn't go down too well with Sapphire.

"He wasn't…" She trails off and hugs her arms across her body, frowning a little. "He wasn't what I expected."

Anxiety ripples through my chest. She doesn't sound like she hates him. *What the hell did he do to her in there?*

"What?" I bite out. "He wasn't an evil and black-hearted monster?"

Her eyes cut sharply to mine, though I try to remain focused on the road. "I didn't say that."

"Then what *are* you saying?"

I don't know why I'm pressing the issue. Even though she met with him hours ago, the image of his pale fingers on her bare skin seems to have branded itself into my brain. I can't stop replaying it, over and over.

All I have to counteract that is one tiny, half-wink.

"He's an expert at mind manipulation, Sapphire. I... was worried." *And I'm damn sure not used to that feeling.*

Her hands drop to her lap and her tone is softer as she says, "I know that. He asked me to be part of his crew."

His crew? If the situation wasn't so serious, I'd break into a laugh.

"What I meant was, he didn't present as a raging, mindless monster. He was... polite. Charming, even. He wanted to explain his side of things."

Cold dread spreads throughout my chest as I realize what she's saying. I've seen it happen before—so many times. To the other members of my pack. To my friends; my kin. My *parents*.

Azriel's whispers—the poison he drips into people's minds. I've seen him turn good people into hollow shadows of their former selves, ready and willing to do his bidding, no matter what that bidding entails.

Sign over your son, Craven, and I will give you and your wife everything.

I push thoughts of my father out of my head and try to concentrate on the present. But if that deadly mind-control has worked on Sapphire as well...

"And?" Somehow, I manage to keep my voice neutral.

Her hands twist in her lap. "I think…"

I don't want her to continue. *Please don't lose yourself to the dark.*

"I think I managed to convince him," she says in a rush.

I almost run off the road in relief.

"It was tough," she says. "He definitely did try some kind of mind trick on me. I felt him probing and pushing; felt myself beginning to cave. But I created a wall around my mind, and I don't believe he sensed it. He thinks he has me."

I could have leaned over and kissed her right there.

I settle for shooting her an approving look. "You're stronger than you appear."

She chuckles. "Damn straight."

My lips twitch upward. "I mean it," I say. "You're stronger than anyone I know. Well done."

"Oh. Well. Thanks." Her cheeks flush a delicate pink, a color that suits her far more than her earlier pallor. She turns away to stare out the window and stays that way until I slow to a halt outside her cottage.

She slowly climbs out of the truck and then turns to lean back in. "You don't mind that I… ran off from your place?"

"I get it. You're used to being independent, and you're a bit of a loner." *Like me.* "I won't be far away, though. Call me if you need me. And, if you have wards up around the house, double check them."

She flashes me a smile so sweet a sudden pain arcs through my chest.

What the hell was that?

"You're a decent hellhound, Caden," she says, her eyes warm. "And a decent man. Thank you. I'll call you when I've had some sleep."

I watch her until she's safely inside.

And I don't drive away for a long time.

The stakes just got a whole hell of a lot higher, and I still don't know how to protect her from the inevitable darkness that is coming for us both.

Sapphire

I WAKE WITH A JOLT. Sunlight streams through the open curtains of my bedroom window and warms my back.

I groan, lifting my head and glancing at the clock on my bedside table.

One-thirty p.m.

I let out another groan and sink face-first back into my pillow. It's soft and warm, and there's nowhere I'd rather be right now. Is it possible to build a pajama day into the schedule, when you're angling to bring down a fallen angel and his demon army?

I look down at myself. Correction. A wrinkled, night-before-dress day.

I must have fallen into bed and asleep before I managed to pull on my PJs. I don't even remember.

A sudden volley of knocking on the front door startles me, and I sit bolt upright. That sound must have been what woke me in the first place. I scramble out of bed, my mind racing. I'm not expecting visitors, and whoever is outside is persistent.

Caden? I catch a glimpse of myself as I pass the mirror and wince. I have enough vanity to hope it isn't him right now. I look a mess—smudged lipstick and my hair a tangled bird's nest. I sigh heavily and wander to the door as another round of knocking begins.

"Okay, okay!" I wrench open the door. "I heard you the first—oh."

Amethyst and Topaz stand on the doorstep, eyeing me with identical expressions of surprise. The former has her arms firmly crossed, and the latter is playing with the topaz ring on her left forefinger.

Their surprise morphs into curiosity. I take a hurried step back as Amethyst strides forward. My wards flare warmly in welcome. They are primed with my blood, and that includes Topaz and Ammie, without question.

"We need to talk," Ammie says in her forthright way, once we are all in the living room.

"By all means." I roll my eyes as Amethyst wanders around.

It looks as if she's searching for something.

"Come in," I add, sarcastically. "Make yourself at home."

Topaz is more apologetic at the intrusion. "Hey, coz."

My gaze softens as I return her smile, before sharpening again when Amethyst picks up my discarded tube of lipstick from the mantelpiece.

She arches an eyebrow. "Late night?"

I scuttle over and snatch the lipstick off her, my cheeks burning. "None of your business."

Amethyst's eyes widen, before she heads to my bedroom and pokes her head inside. Upon my splutter of annoyance, she walks back to the lounge and drops down onto the couch.

"Sorry." She looks up at me, slightly embarrassed. "I had to make sure we were alone."

I shake my head in disbelief. "Who did you think... ah. Caden."

"Well, you know." Ammie shrugs. "I haven't met him, but if he's anything like Dane..."

"Or Kyan," Topaz pipes up, sliding onto the couch between Ammie and me.

"He's nothing like them," I confirm, but a tiny pang of something that feels like guilt niggles at me.

He's as hot as hell, and your witchy private bits would be very happy if he wanted to take things further.

I ignore my traitorous thoughts and ask, "Why are you here?"

"It's the Fae," Topaz says, her voice grave. "We have updates."

TEN MINUTES LATER, I'm curled up in the armchair in my favorite dressing gown, having taken the world's fastest shower. Amethyst and Topaz take up the sofa opposite me. Three steaming cups of peppermint tea brewed by my sister are clustered on the coffee table between us.

The run-of-the-mill domesticity makes me want to laugh.

"Okay, I'm ready now," I say. "Lay it on me."

"The Fae are planning to hold a summit." Topaz picks up her tea, cradling it between her hands before taking a sip. "There's going to be an amendment to the Accord. This time, they're going after the celestials. They're going to try and get them to sign."

"When you say, 'they'..."

"Everyone," Tee says, nodding at my wide-eyed look. "I can hardly believe it myself. The celestials wouldn't sign last time round, all those years ago. Said they were above the petty dealings of us lesser species scuttling around on earth. But all the species that have been spoken to so far are in agreement. The celestials need to somehow be persuaded to sign the Accord, which will hopefully give some level of security around the continued existence of this planet."

"Holy goddess."

"I know." Amethyst sounds as shocked as me, and she must have known this information before arriving today. "It took some convincing, but Captain Orion finally managed to get some of the Fae on the Accord Council to listen."

Captain Orion? I mouth my query at Topaz.

She rolls her eyes at my questioning look. "She has two Fae friends, apparently. Orion as well as Aveen. She won't shut up about them."

"Hey!"

I laugh. "Doesn't your friendship with Queen Maewen and King Rhodri of the Winter Court trump that, Tee?"

Topaz joins my laughter. "Well, *I* think so, but Ammie says the Summer Court is a harder nut to crack than Winter. She may be right."

I'm impressed with Ammie in spite of myself. The Summer Fae are notoriously secretive; they aren't known to consort with humans on a regular basis.

Which means things must be getting bad.

"The celestials have never listened before," I point out. "What's changed? Why do the Fae think they'll listen now?"

Topaz and Amethyst exchange a look. Chills run through me. I already know the answer to my question before Topaz says anything.

"Azriel." Her fingers tighten around her mug, knuckles whitening against the ceramic. "They know he's here, and they know about the cracks in the ether. A celestial in our world, even a fallen one, is dangerous for everyone, even them. They don't meddle in human affairs, usually, but this is different. This is one of their own, and his presence here potentially affects every celestial."

I nibble on my lower lip, thoughts whirling. I wish I had my cousin's optimism.

"Azriel fell centuries ago," I whisper. "Technically, he's not a celestial. Not anymore."

"Well," Amethyst says, turning her gaze to the window with a finality that leaves me cold. "Let's hope the Accord Council can come up with something. Because if they don't, the Fae are ready for war."

War?

It's a totally alien concept. Thanks to the Accord, we have grown up in a time of relative peace between the magical species. There is always some species-ism, unfortunately, given the nature of humans and some supes, but war? No.

I can't imagine the chaos that would result from an all-out magical war. If the Council fails in their mission to get the celestials on side...

I'm so caught up in the dawning realization that our world might be on the brink of war, that I entirely miss what Amethyst says next. Only the anger in Topaz's voice jolts me back to the present moment.

"You can't be serious."

"I have to know," Amethyst says firmly. "Topaz, it's the only way. I have to be sure."

Something about the way Topaz is glaring at my sister—so at odds with her usual calm demeanor—has me leaning forward.

"What did I miss?" I cut between their staring contest, and they both turn to me.

"I need to dream travel again." Amethyst taps her mug, at odds with her confident tone. "I might be able to find out what Azriel is planning. If he's heard about the summit, he could decide to show his face there. If I dream walk, I could possibly find out."

"No *way*," Topaz exclaims. "You're not going through that again, Ammie. Remember what happened last time?"

Images of dead bodies and smoke-blackened trees around the Aurora Spa Resort fill my mind. The terror on the faces of battle-hardened shifters still remains with me, as do the deadly whispers from demon wraiths in the darkness. The threat of death and destruction, of everything I hold dear, rises alongside a surge of nausea in my belly.

"No, Ammie." I shiver. "I agree with Tee on this one."

"But I have to take the risk." "Amethyst sets down her mug and folds her arms over her middle. "It's the only way."

"It isn't the only way." I surprise both of them. "I have something in train. Just... wait a couple of days. Please?"

Amethyst's eyes narrow. "What do you have 'in train'?"

How can I tell her, without both of them losing their shit?

"I've been working on something, and I think it is going to pan out. Just... trust me. For once in your lives, please. Trust me." My gaze cuts downward, to the floor. It feels strange keeping secrets from them. I shift on the couch, their twin gazes weighing me down.

"A couple of days? Do we have that leeway?" Topaz sounds doubtful, but at least she is considering what I said.

I raise my chin back up to look her directly in the eyes. "I will find out about Azriel. Just... promise me. Two days."

"Sapph..." Ammie's voice is soft, a stark contrast to her previous impatience. "We do trust you. But we worry."

"I know."

"Does this have anything to do with that hellhound shifter?"

"His name is Caden, and he is helping me with... something."

"Something?" Topaz's tone is wry, and I glare at her.

"Wait," Ammie says. "The lipstick? The rumpled dress? Is that why you missed your jewelry workshop yesterday? Because you're running around after some hellhound?"

Something snaps inside my chest, and I round on her. "That is so hypocritical! Both of you have been doing the same thing, but I'm not *allowed?*"

"That's different, and you know it."

The two of us glare at each other. Topaz releases a deep sigh.

"I think what Amethyst is trying to say is..." She trails off, brows drawing together as if even *she* doesn't quite know what Ammie means. "Working with hellhounds is one thing. But using one to get to Azriel himself? Sapph, you're playing with fire."

I include her in my glare. "I am asking you both to trust me. Two days. That's what I'm asking for. Will you grant me that time?"

After several charged seconds, Ammie nods, followed by Topaz.

Before they leave, Topaz gives me a tight hug. Amethyst looks like she's ready to storm out without acknowledging me, but at the last moment she pulls me into her arms.

"I do love you," she whispers. "Fiercely."

"Yes, I know. Love you, too, sis."

She gives me one last squeeze before hurrying out the door.

Once I'm alone, I don't know what to do with myself. I end up making toast and eating it on the back porch, watching the colors of the sky shift as late afternoon draws in. A chill wind ruffles through my hair, and I retrieve a blanket from my bedroom, fingering the soft knit and thinking about Caden.

It's a rare moment of peace, sitting vigil over the quiet, empty garden. I think about the humans going about their business, blissfully ignorant of the turmoil that might unfold around them in the near future.

None of us will be left unscathed, if the world goes to war.

I find myself scrolling aimlessly through my phone, before my thumb hovers over Caden's name. After a minute of deliberation, I press the button, and then hold up the phone to my ear.

It barely has a chance to ring once before Caden's terse response comes through on the other end.

"Sapphire."

Relief blazes through me at the sound of his voice.

"Are you all right?"

My hands tremble as I fumble with the phone, switching it to my other ear. Suddenly, I want him here with me. My free hand curls in the blanket as I nod, before remembering he can't see me. "Yes, yes, I'm fine."

There's a pause. "You don't sound fine. Want me to come over?"

I bite down on my bottom lip. "Yes, thanks."

Barely fifteen minutes later, the loud noise of a motorbike rumbles up and cuts off.

I place my hand on the porch railing and send magic through the house wards, conjuring up an image of Caden— his physical form, his scent, and the way he moves when he walks—and letting the wards know he is safe. He should now be recognizable to the protection magic crisscrossing the property.

Caden strides around the side of the cottage and steps up onto the porch. He drops down beside me with casual ease. I don't ask how he knew I was out back. His eyes land on the blanket I'm wrapped in, but he doesn't comment on it.

"I have some news, and it wasn't safe to tell you over the phone." It's a plausible explanation for me to want him here, even if it's only half the truth. "Did you know that the

Fae are planning a summit to discuss changes to the Accord?"

Surprise flashes across Caden's face.

"I'll take that as a no, then." I fiddle with the edge of the blanket. "Which probably means that Azriel doesn't know, either."

"How do *you* know?"

I explain about Topaz and Amethyst's unexpected visit. He listens patiently, taking it all in. When I get to the part about Amethyst's plan to do more dream walking, his gaze slants sideways to meet mine.

"Remarkable." He shakes his head. "I knew you were all powerful—Kyan made that clear—but your sister's talents sound almost as impressive as yours."

I flush under the indirect praise, dropping my gaze to my knees. "I don't know about that. Anyway, I want her to wait. It's too dangerous. Last time, Azriel almost killed her."

Caden nods. He seems unsurprised by the revelation. He's a hellhound, after all; I'm certain he's seen more death than most.

"I have a favor to ask." I swallow, uncertain. "Could you find out what Azriel knows? My sister is... contrary. She's not going to wait around for long. She promised me two days, but knowing her, the clock started ticking at midnight last night."

Caden's jaw flexes. His expression is unreadable as he studies the darkening sky above us. Then his warm palm lands on my shoulder.

"I've got your back, Sapph. I'll see what I can do."

I'm momentarily distracted, both by the contact, and his shortened version of my name. There is something strangely intimate about a nickname, and it makes me want to reply in kind.

But what do I call him? *Cade? Den?* I'm not used to this kind of thing.

He jumps to his feet and leaves me not long after, dropping soundlessly off the edge of the porch and disappearing from sight.

I watch the sunset from my spot outside, heedless of the drop in temperature. It's beautiful, but my mind is far, far away. When will the Council decide? How will they get the celestials to the table to even talk, let alone consider signing?

I can't help wondering how Topaz and Amethyst are doing now, and if Ammie is planning to go ahead with the dream walking, regardless of my pleas. My mind wanders to Caden, out there somewhere, hopefully making good on his promise.

I've got your back.

Other than Amethyst and Topaz, no one has ever had my back before now.

Once night falls, the chill in the air gets the better of me, and I head inside, but my thoughts continue to swirl.

I have the strong impression that we are all running out of time to save the world.

WHEN I WAKE in total darkness, my first thought is: *Shit. My sleeping pattern is shot to hell.*

At least, that's what I initially blame for my sudden jolt into consciousness. But then a strange scraping noise from the corner of the room makes me stiffen.

My breathing grows shallow but the noise has gone. Was it even there? Is it simply my imagination, working overtime?

I strain my eyesight, but I can't see a thing, other than half shapes of furniture that look familiar and yet not, coated as they are in black shadow.

Is this Azriel's doing?

How did he get in, past my wards?

"Hello?" I whisper.

No response.

Goddess, I'm acting insane.

I flop back down on the mattress, chastising myself for being so easily spooked. I grab my phone and check the time. It's not even one a.m. The stress of the last few weeks must really be getting to me.

As I put down my phone, readying to sleep again, something moves in the shadows. I don't have time to react, beyond a half-scream that bubbles up my throat.

My voice is harshly cut off by a set of clawed hands. A wave of terror floods over me. I'm sure it must be Azriel, come to finish me off.

I thrash beneath the claws, determined not to give in without a fight. The dark figure has long hair that brushes against my face, some of the strands crawling into my mouth. I spit out the hair and push, hard, winning a small reprieve that enables me to jump properly out of bed and land on my feet. Then the creature is on me again, wrestling and clawing and growling. I don't even have time to call up my magic. All I can do is fend it off, dodging the deadly swipe as it tries to slash my throat, kicking and punching as I try to avoid being killed. When we stagger into a shard of moonlight, I realize that what I'd taken for claws are actually obscenely long nails.

My attacker is female. My surprise makes me fumble. She pushes me backward onto the mattress, jumping on top and straddling me. She bares her teeth and growls at me; in the darkness, they glint menacingly, as do those absurd nails.

"Not so tough now, huh?" she hisses. "Bitch."

I buck upwards with my hips, trying to throw her off, but she's much stronger than I am, and too heavy to easily dislodge. She's impressively strong, actually. Stronger than her slim frame would suggest.

It's then that I catch sight of her eyes—crimson and filled with blood lust. *She's a hellhound.* She may not have shifted—yet—but rage is driving her, and the unbridled hatred in that expression makes my blood run cold.

Wildly, I think back to our visit to Azriel's mansion, remembering the woman who answered the door, with her long, snaking braid and judgmental expression.

"Bet you thought I wouldn't find out." Her fingers tighten

around my neck. I scrabble for purchase, but it's no use. Her grip is vicelike and merciless. "How naïve."

What are you talking about? I want to scream.

Is this to do with Azriel? Or something else? This feels personal.

Black spots begin to cloud my vision. Unconsciousness threatens to pull me under in a matter of seconds if I don't do something fast.

You are a Redferne. A mage. You have more power in one of your fingertips than this hellhound bitch has in all of her stupid, over-grown nails. You are not going to die like this.

With every fiber of my remaining strength, I give her a mental shove. My magic burns hot and bright deep within me. The room is filled with searing white light.

My lungs expand with oxygen as her weight flies off me, and I sit up, choking and spluttering. I blink into the darkness and massage my throat with both hands, before leaning across and flicking the switch on my bedside lamp. My veins tingle with adrenaline. I raise my arm, dimly noting the ripples of magic that flow beneath the surface of my skin.

I draw my knees up to my chest and hug them, rocking back and forth, gathering my breath before turning my head to stare at the far wall. The intruder is slumped there in an unconscious pile, her head to one side and her limbs spread-eagled. She looks like a broken doll.

It seems that my burst of instinctual magic was a little too effective.

Oops.

Finally, I gather the courage to approach her. My pulse is racing. Part of me thinks her eyes might fly open and her hands will grab me as soon as I get within range.

But when I press two fingers to her neck, she doesn't move.

I can feel a faint, thready pulse, so she's definitely still alive. She's simply out cold.

I collapse to the floor beside her, gaping at her, trying to catch up with what just happened.

Now what?

It's the middle of the night. I have no idea where my sister is, and even if I did... I don't want her to worry. Or, even worse, have a reason to try dream walking again.

A bubble of hysteria rises up in my throat.

Eventually, despite my reluctance, I do the only thing I *can* think of.

I call Caden.

HE ARRIVES IN RECORD TIME.

Is he hanging around the neighborhood? Keeping an eye on me? The thought both comforts and irritates me in equal measure. I can look after myself. Tonight has proven that, clearly enough.

Nevertheless, when I open the door and let him in, I have to fight the urge to fling my arms around his neck. Ruse or no ruse—all this time we've been spending together pretending to be in a relationship has got my wires crossed.

Get it together. Just because he's acting like your boyfriend, doesn't mean he is. Remember your mission.

"Through here." I mumble, awkward. "I woke up, and she was just... there. She attacked me, with no provocation. She must have climbed in through the window or something. Though how she got through—"

I break off. I sent a picture through the wards earlier, of a safe hellhound shifter with dark hair, pale skin, and green-crimson eyes. Did I specify *which* hellhound was allowed in...

Damn.

I make a mental note to adjust the wards, limiting them specifically to Caden, and perhaps Dane and Kyan, as soon as I've finished dealing with this crazy woman.

"She was very angry. Kept saying I was naïve to think she wouldn't find out."

"Ah." Caden says nothing more, but simply follows me through to the bedroom in silence. When he peers in and sees the woman lying in a heap on the floor, he huffs out a breath that sounds faintly annoyed.

"You know her?" I ask.

My mind is running a mile a minute. Who is she? One of Azriel's followers? Has she figured out who Caden and I really are, or has she turned traitor? Maybe Azriel changed his mind about me. Did he send her here to kill me?

Caden sets his jaw. He looks like he'd rather be anywhere else but right here. His eyes dart away from mine, then back again.

"I do." He forces out the next words with obvious reluctance. "She's my ex-girlfriend."

I just stare at him. "Your... ex-girlfriend."

"Yes," Caden grits out. He runs a hand over his face, looking tired. "We broke up several months ago."

"I see." A million questions flood my mind. I sink heavily onto the end of the bed, weighed down with the shock of it all. "So, she's not... this isn't Azriel's doing?"

"I very much doubt it." Caden glares at the opposite wall, as if he needs to release some strong emotion but doesn't know where to direct it.

I know how he feels.

"You're going to have to do better than that."

To my surprise, he sits down on the bed beside me. Although he keeps a conservative distance, I'm hyper-aware of his proximity. Irritated, I keep my focus on the woman in front of us. She's still out cold, but her chest is rising and falling more evenly now, which I take to be a good sign.

"She was the one who let us in at Azriel's place," Caden murmurs.

"I remember her. Long braid. Nice dress. She *sniffed* me."

His lips twitch. "She did. Most likely she smelt my scent on you, and vice versa. I guess she took it personally."

"You guess?" My palms tingle as my irritation blossoms into full-blown annoyance. My chest feels hot as I look down at the unconscious woman.

She's very striking, in the way that hellhound shifters tend to be, with her pale skin, full lips, and waterfall of shiny black hair.

It's no surprise that Caden wanted to be with her.

I clench and release my fists. *Jealous,* I realize with a shock. *I'm jealous.*

"What happened?" I ask, dragging my gaze away from her and onto Caden. He's watching me with interest. "Why did you break up?"

Something flutters behind his eyes. He stands abruptly, shoving his hands deep into his pockets.

"That's classified information."

Classified? Another wave of anger rolls over me, stronger than before. I head to my bedroom door and gesture pointedly through the opening. "Get out."

He just looks confused.

Unbelievable.

"I was jumped in my *sleep* and almost *choked to death* by some crazy ex of yours." I fold my arms. Magic surges through my chest, fueling the fire in my belly. "If you're not going to tell me what happened, then I recommend you leave —before I knock *you* out cold, too."

He stares at me, saying nothing.

"Get out, Caden, and take your girlfr—"

"Things ended badly between us." Caden cuts me off before I can go further. I fall quiet, one hand against the doorframe. "I was the one to call it quits. She... she wanted us to try again. Kept approaching me, and every time, I've made it clear I am not interested."

There's a pause, in which I stare down at the floor. Why does it matter so much, what happened between Caden and this woman?

I feel the warmth of his body close to mine. He must have moved across the carpet in that silent way shifters have; he doesn't touch me at all, but the hairs on the back of my neck stand up.

"So, she thinks I've come along and..." *Stolen her man?* I swallow. When I look up, he's gazing at me intently.

"Lucia has never been one to give up easily," he murmurs. "But I had no idea she'd go this far. I'll talk to her when she wakes up. Make sure this doesn't happen again."

I glance around him at the figure on the floor, coming to a decision. "Don't bother. I can handle it. Now that I'm awake."

"Then why did you even bother calling me?"

I glare at him. "I don't know. A moment of stupidity?"

Caden scowls and we size each other up. I don't know why I'm so angry with him. It isn't his fault his ex broke into my house and tried to kill me.

I take a few deep breaths and release them slowly. His scowl clears, though he still seems uneasy.

"Are you sure, Sapph? She can be pretty cray-cray." He taps the side of his temple.

"No shit." I turn on my heel, and he follows me out of the bedroom. He moves slowly, reluctantly. "I've got this, Caden. I knocked her out once, and I'll do it again if I have to."

His jaw flexes, and he casts one brooding look back

toward the bedroom before stalking over to the exit. He puts one hand on the door handle, and then glances back at me.

"All right." His eyes narrow and his voice is like gravel. "Call me if she tries anything more."

The door slams shut behind him, signaling his displeasure with my decision.

Too bad.

I let out a sigh and turn back toward my bedroom.

This night has begun to seem endless. I shiver as I pass the window, hoping for the first rays of dawn to pierce the horizon, but it's many hours off, yet.

I steel myself before I cross the threshold. Facing an aggressive hellhound shifter alone—even an unconscious one —is suddenly a daunting prospect.

The night isn't over. Not by a long shot.

"Ouch!"

I drop the bunch of dried sage onto the countertop and cradle my burned wrist with my free hand, hopping up and down a couple of times before turning down the flame on the gas cooktop. The tincture I'm brewing bubbles sluggishly in the saucepan, and I glare at it.

Brewing is not my forte.

"Where's Amethyst when you need her?" I mutter, picking up the sage again and dropping a few leaves into the pan. Purple smoke starts mushrooming into the kitchen, and I swear, grabbing a wooden spoon and mixing frantically. "She's always around to poke her nose in when I *don't* want to see her..."

Eventually, I manage to get the purple-tinted liquid that I'm after. It's still smoking a bit too much for my liking, but it'll have to do.

I pour the contents of the saucepan into a bowl and carry it into my bedroom. As soon as I kneel down beside Lucia, the doubts creep into my mind.

What if she goes for me again? Despite what I said to

Caden, I got lucky last time. There's no telling what she'll do when she wakes.

I shove the bowl underneath her nose and wait.

It doesn't take long for the tincture to work. Her nose twitches, and her eyelids flutter gently. I remove the bowl and sit back on my heels.

Slowly, her eyes open.

My first impression wasn't wrong. She truly is beautiful to look at. Like Snow White in her glass coffin, stirring into consciousness. The serenity that graces her delicate features doesn't last, however; as soon as her gaze lands on me, her eyes narrow.

"You..." she slurs. "What the hell did you do to me, witch?"

I brace a hand against her shoulder as she struggles to prop herself up onto her elbows. "Hey, take it easy."

"Don't touch me, you bitch!"

Witch? Or bitch? I resist the urge to roll my eyes.

She hisses, and I drop my hand away.

"You almost cracked my head open."

"Yeah, after you tried to *kill* me," I shoot back. It's no use; I can feel my self-control slipping away. "And after breaking into my house, I might add!"

Lucia huffs. Her green eyes are still a bit glazed, like she's shaking off the effects of my magic surge. "Kill you? No way. I only came here to warn you."

"Warn me?"

"To keep your *whore* hands off Caden."

As she speaks, she struggles up to a sitting position. Her lips peel back, revealing a perfect row of white teeth. I move away and sit on the bed, facing her.

"He isn't your property."

"He's my *destiny*." Her eyes glitter. "We're alike, me and him. Meant for each other. Sooner or later, he'll realize that."

She picks at a non-existent thread on the hem of her dress, before arching an eyebrow my way. "Pity. If you hadn't come along and *ruined* everything for him, he'd be by my side later tonight. Where he belongs."

I take in the crushed velvet bodice that she's wearing. The black lacquered nails and spiked heels. The short, figure-hugging skirt.

My heart starts thumping harder. "And where does he *belong*, exactly?"

"Only the most loyal of Azriel's followers were chosen." Lucia trails an idle hand down her thigh. She seems deep in thought, like she's forgotten I'm in the room. "The bravest, the strongest. The best of the best. That *should* have included Caden."

She's back with me again, her eyes narrowing in slits. "A blood ritual for a fallen celestial. By the time dawn breaks, you have *no idea* the kind of power he'll have. The kind of power we all will have."

I stare at her in shock. Without warning, she lunges at me. My arms come up, casting a shield charm before I'm even conscious of doing so.

She hits the shield and falls back with an exasperated growl. I eye her warily.

Play dumb.

"Caden doesn't know about this?" I let a tinge of hurt slip into my voice, making it seem as if I'm heartbroken for him. Anguished that my "boyfriend" may have fallen out of Azriel's favor. But my mind is racing.

"All thanks to you. Azriel doesn't trust Caden at the moment." She gets to her feet, smooth and graceful now, looking down at me with disdain. Her triumph at my defeat radiates off her in waves.

"Get out." This time, when my voice trembles, I don't try and stop it. It's not entirely an act, after all. "Get out of my house!"

With one final glare, Lucia turns and slips out of the room, vanishing into the shadows. I wait for a full minute in the silence, sending out feelers to every corner of the cottage to ensure she really is gone, before I grab my phone and dial Caden's number. Again.

Caden

WHEN SAPPHIRE RUNS out of the cottage, her face is flushed and her eyes glitter feverishly, even in the darkness. She dashes toward my car and lets herself in without preamble, her long hair tumbling over her shoulders as she settles into the passenger seat.

I have to tell myself not to stare as I turn the key in the ignition. She's talking a mile a minute about Lucia and some blood ritual she mentioned on the phone. I wait until we're on the main road before I cut her off and try to make sense of the flood of information.

"I've never heard of such a ritual before."

Why would such information have passed me by? Is this something new? And the fact that I've been excluded from the event itself is a concern. If it was Azriel who chose the attendees, then I have clearly fallen out of favor —most likely because I introduced Sapphire as Sophie. I can't think of anything else I've done recently to cause doubt.

"He must have found a way to strengthen his power." Sapphire groans, frustrated. "We should go. I want to see what we're up against."

A prickle of unease runs through me. "Something isn't right about this."

She shoots me a grim look. "I know. All the more reason to check it out, I'd say."

"We don't even know where the ritual will be held."

"I was thinking we could start with that black lake and..." She breaks off, staring over my shoulder. "All right. Well, we do now."

I swivel my head and follow her line of sight. Several miles ahead of us, on the dark hill to my left, is a string of glittering lights traveling slowly along the edge of a ridge. They bob and sway, as if lanterns are being carried by people walking on uneven ground. There must be close to a hundred of them. It looks like the line is headed toward the summit.

The sky above the hilltop is glowing with a green-tinged, silvery light. It is not a light that generally comes from nature, unless you count the aurora phenomenon, but this glow does not have a natural feel. Nor is this man-made. This kind of power—and the buzzing supernatural feel that permeates the air around us—can only come from one thing.

A celestial.

I DRIVE ON, toward the mouth of a narrow gully, and then the road begins to climb. I slow down and dip the headlights so we don't draw attention to ourselves. Most of the bobbing lights are high up on the cliff above the road, but I'm taking no chances.

The closer we get, the paler Sapphire becomes. Her shoulders hunch inwards, like she's withdrawing into herself. I ask her repeatedly if she wants to turn back.

"I'm fine." She waves her hand with an air of impatience after the fourth time I ask. "I just... I've got a bad feeling, and the closer we get, the more unwell I feel."

She clutches her stomach, and I'm tempted to ignore her and turn the car around at the next pull off we reach.

She clears her throat and says, "I'm not sure why, but I need to be here tonight. It's part of my power—to know things. Not that my magic ever gives me the full picture, mind you." Her chuckle is faint. "Very frustrating, at times."

"I bet." Okay. So, we won't be turning back. I don't want to argue with witch magic.

I drive as close to the top of the ridge as I dare, before drawing to a halt and tucking the car in behind some straggling bushes. It isn't full cover, but the darkness and the distraction of the ritual might be enough. Especially if we travel the rest of the way on foot.

We creep through the brush, my shifter eyesight providing a smooth way forward even in the dark. Sapphire follows closely behind. We find an outcrop of rocks that gives us a good vantage point of the summit, without being in the direct path in or out, and settle in to watch.

Sapphire shivers, crouched next to me, and I automatically put my arm across her shoulders and draw her in to my side. She snuggles close, as if in need of my body warmth, but I doubt her shivering relates to being cold.

I'm almost as nervous as she is. What is about to happen? If this ritual is designed to increase Azriel's already formidable power, then who or what will be able to stop him, if the ritual is successful?

Sapphire twists and brings her mouth close to my ear.

"I'll cast a shield to hide our scent and mute our voices," she whispers, so quiet I only just catch the words.

I nod approval. No way, with this many shifters swarming all over the hill, would we be able to avoid discovery without some kind of intervention.

She makes a small motion with her hand and says, "Done."

Strange that I can't feel anything around us. I push with my hellhound senses, but... nothing.

"How loud can we talk?" I mouth, and she smiles briefly in the darkness.

"Normally."

I catch sight of several faces as they wander past our hiding place. I don't recognize any of them. Some features are narrow and pointed, some broad and burly. These are not just hellhound shifters, as I first thought when Sapphire called me. There are wolves, coyotes, bears, foxes, and even a lynx, wending their way up the incline to the summit. There are so many of them—even more than the number of lights indicated, as not everyone is holding a lantern.

Some of the shifters are dressed for the occasion in long robes of velvet and silk, with glints of silver and gold at their throats. Others are in dark nondescript clothing, or ordinary street clothes. The only unifying aspect of the gathering seems to be the glittering excitement on the faces of Azriel's followers.

"Hey." I turn to Sapphire, still keeping my voice as low as I can. Despite her magical shield, I don't want to take any chances. What I do want is to erase the worried line between her brows and ease the tightness of her mouth. Her pinched expression is making my chest ache, so I try to lighten the mood with conversation. "What sort of shifter do you think that guy is?"

She follows my gaze toward a couple who has just passed us. The female is half the male's size but clearly the one in charge, judging by the way he scurries after her, trying to keep up. Both of them look eager for whatever is coming.

"Hmm." She frowns in concentration. "A wolf?"

I shake my head. "Coyote."

She arches an eyebrow at me, her silent question clear. *How do you know?*

I settle back on my haunches. It looks like we'll be here for a while; we might as well get comfortable in our little protected bubble. "The scent. Plus, see his eyes?"

Sapphire arches her neck, just in time to catch a flash of his amber gaze as he stares around, before he and the woman disappear from sight. "Damn, you're good."

"I know shifters." I shrug. "It's my world, after all, and it's my job to know who I'm dealing with."

"Must be nice." Sapphire rests her head against my shoulder, her tone wistful. "Being part of a pack. Knowing exactly who you're supposed to be. Having so many others around you who... understand."

"I suppose so. But it has its downsides."

Sapphire looks askance at me, but I don't meet her gaze. The memory of Azriel's takeover is too fresh. The bond I shared with my pack, our old unity... my parents.

Everything I knew and loved was shattered in the blink of an eye.

The truth is, I have no pack. Not anymore.

"I'd like to know I always have someone to fall back on," Sapphire says. "Shifters are lucky that way. You're never alone. Not for a second."

"You're not alone. You're part of a coven, aren't you? What about your sister and cousin?"

Her mouth curves up into a warm smile. I'm temporarily distracted by the shape of it. "Of course, they're there when I need them, and often when I don't." She scrunches up her nose, and I can't help smiling. "But it's not the same. Most of the time, I'm hundreds of miles away from them. Maybe it's selfish, but I guess I want more. I want... somewhere I can belong."

Something shifts inside me at her words. I want the same thing; it's all I've ever wanted.

Our faces are close together. I don't know how but here

we are. Breathing the same air, anticipating. On the verge of something bigger.

Those sweet, luscious lips have haunted me since the night we met. I remember with perfect detail—the hungry way she kissed me, the feel of her body beneath mine, the sound of her moans as I touched her...

Her breath ghosts over my face. I let her take the lead as she fits her small palm against my jaw, readying to draw my face down to hers.

Before our mouths can meet, she stiffens. I pull back in alarm. My eyes scan her face; she's turned so pale she looks almost incandescent. Her gaze drifts beyond me, toward the hilltop.

I turn my head with dread already filling my belly. I don't need her to tell me what I already know in my bones.

Azriel has arrived.

14

A *BOOM* ECHOES over the hillside, like a clap of thunder.

The sky above us pulses. That same eerie green light from earlier snakes down from the clouds and through the crowd, curling around them all, then drifting away into the shadows.

Nausea rises as I imagine the terrible scenario—Azriel reigning over the world, suffocating all of us with his eternal quest for glory, until nothing is left but darkness and ash.

The fallen angel is easy to pick out among the crowd. He stands on a rocky outcrop above the heads of the gathered crowd. When he appears, the assembly bows their heads in unison. For a few moments, the noise and chatter dies down. There is silence from the dark huddled mass worshipping in front of Azriel.

Then two demons step up behind Azriel, standing at his elbow, one on each side. Whatever they are standing on is slightly lower than their boss, no doubt to affirm both support and subservience in equal measure.

Sapphire hisses in a breath. "That's... Is that... *Luthor?*"

I study the demons. The one on Azriel's left is unfamiliar,

but the one on the right... "Yes. I've seen him before, but not for a while. A soul collector. How do you know him?"

"He was the one trying to harvest Topaz's soul. She showed me and Ammie his image once, in a scrying bowl."

"Ah."

Luthor's gaze rakes the crowd, but luckily, he doesn't seem to be looking this way. Thank all that is holy for Sapphire's shield, giving us at least some semblance of privacy.

All noise dies down then, and the only sound I can hear, apart from Sapph's and my shallow breathing, is the wind whistling across the ridge and through the trees.

Then Azriel speaks, his voice ringing out over the heads of the bowed crowd. "I thank you all."

Sapphire shudders, as if the voice itself is cause for horror. Perhaps it is. Perhaps I have gotten too used to it, over the years.

"For your loyalty in coming here tonight. You have proven yourselves most useful over the past several months."

The crowd murmurs as if in reverence, the shadows among them shifting and rippling like a black sea.

"But..." Azriel lifts a hand, silencing them with the gesture. "The time has come for me to say farewell. There is a final task for you to perform, and I need each and every one of you to do your part. Tonight."

He has them spellbound, caught up in the rapture of listening to his speech. From the corner of my eye, I catch sight of the green mist from earlier creeping around the perimeter of the scene. It's hazy, but gathering, solidifying quickly, forming a barrier between us and them.

Above the mist, Azriel's face stretches into a broad grin. Even from this distance, the expression makes my blood run cold; his pallor, the dark pools where his eyes look like holes in his head; the glint of his sharp teeth.

"Let the blood ritual begin."

A tendril of mist reaches out, grabbing one of the shifter women and lifting her into the air several feet away from Azriel. Then another tendril grabs a male and lifts him up on the other side of the crowd. Azriel raises a hand and makes a sharp movement as if slashing something with his fingernails. Across the sea of worshippers, both the man and the woman's throats burst open and blood pours out, splattering the ground and everyone below them in bright red blood.

The crowd gapes and then, as one, begins to scream as tendrils of mist grab them, one after the other.

Is he going to kill them all? Surely not. There are *hundreds* here...

Over the ensuing chaos, I glimpse Azriel's face. He revels in the horror, grinning ever wider as his mist snatches one shifter after another and slaughters them with ease. The demons behind him watch with glee as people push and scramble over each other in their haste to escape. They can't. The green mist has trapped them in place.

Sapphire clamps her fingers on my forearm. She's already on her feet, her face ashen, readying to scramble over the rocks hiding us.

"*No.*" I pull her back, sick to my stomach. "You go up there, Sapph. You'll die."

"We have to do *something*!" Her gaze is horror-filled. "We have to help them!"

Another piercing scream fills the air, rising above the already horrific shrieks and cries, and my breath catches in my throat. I swallow down the bile that has risen.

Lucia is likely in that crowd. And as much as she annoyed me, no one deserves to die like that.

How can I stop this, and still keep Sapphire safe?

Sapphire jumps out from our hiding place and runs toward the greedy, swirling mist.

"No!" I sprint after her and grab her round the waist,

throwing her over my shoulder. My mind is in a whirl. I can't think of what is happening behind us; I have to concentrate on one thing—getting her out of there to safety.

She screams as I run, bashing her fists on my back, but I don't stop till I reach the car and throw her through to the passenger seat from the driver's side. I slide inside and grip her arm again before she can scurry out the other door.

"I will. Not. Let. You. Die." My teeth are clenched, the pain of suppressing my grief hurting my chest.

Some of those shifters will be people I know. People I once called my pack.

Growls rise up from my chest, and Sapphire buries her face in her hands and sobs. I throw the car into gear and accelerate away from the carnage as fast as I can.

I don't let go of Sapphire.

"Please, Caden. You need to turn back. What are you doing?"

I ignore her. The car lurches around, half off the road and into the gravel before I manage to right it. The engine screams in protest under my rough handling.

"They're *dying!*" she says, her voice forlorn.

"Yes. And if we turn back, you'll die right along with them. I can't stop him, up there. So, I'm doing the only thing I can. I'm trying to keep you safe."

And in doing so, I've just left people I know to be butchered.

I pray that the scene of carnage we left behind was enough to keep Azriel and his minions from noticing our less-than-subtle departure.

A loud *boom* shakes the earth around us, seeming to come from within the ground itself.

Sapphire grips the edge of her seat. "Let go of my arm."

"You'll try to go back. And you'll die."

"*Caden!*"

Before I can say anything, silver-white light erupts from Sapphire, flooding through the car in a hot, blinding wave, engulfing me with its intensity. I release her arm and swerve wildly, temporarily blinded, before somehow regaining control of the wheel.

When the light fades, Sapphire is slumped in her seat, panting heavily. She raises a trembling hand and runs it through her disheveled hair.

My mind is buzzing, blank with shock.

I grip the steering wheel so hard I'm surprised it doesn't shatter.

Sapphire mumbles an apology before her lips clamp together in a thin slashing line, but I can tell she is shocked. And embarrassed.

I can barely see the road ahead of us anymore; I'm still half-blinded by that flash.

She's sits there, mouth clamped shut, like she has no idea of the importance of what just happened.

Impossible.

She has to know. The truth is undeniable, staring both of us straight in the face. I just witnessed it with my own eyes.

Sapphire has celestial light magic.

Sapphire

CADEN CONTINUES TO DRIVE, white-knuckled around the steering wheel, his jaw locked tight. His face is like thunder.

Why did he force the issue? Why would he not go back?

I glance in the side mirror. The hillside is shrinking with each passing second, the horror fading into the distance.

"I could have saved some of them," I say.

His fists flex against the wheel as the car careens along the highway back in the direction of home. My home. His gaze lands on me, and I have to fight to hold my head high. I've never seen him so angry—his eyes are crimson, not green. The rage pierces right through me without mercy.

"We agreed to *stake out* the ritual." He snarls. "Watching you die wasn't part of the plan. You saw what that was—a bloodbath. If we'd stuck around, we would've been next."

"You don't know that," I snap back at him. "Besides, it wasn't your call to make. You should have trusted me to know my own limits. To know what my magic is capable of."

"Not my call? Kyan charged me with *protecting* you, Sapphire. To do that, I had to leave behind people I know. People like Lucia, who were likely there in that crowd. I feel their deaths, right here." He takes one hand off the wheel and thumps his chest.

Lucia. And others from his pack? Oh, goddess. Guilt almost overwhelms me.

"You left them... to save me?"

"Yes."

Tears blur my vision as I stare out the windshield. "I'm sorry, Caden. So sorry. I didn't realize..."

I dash away the tears with the back of my hand.

Silence builds, until he bursts out, "Speaking of trust, you've been able to use *light* magic this whole time, and you didn't think it worth mentioning?"

I open my mouth to answer, but when I fully absorb his words, I'm stumped. *Light magic?*

"What are you talking about?"

His eyes flick suspiciously to mine, before his brow furrows. "Wait. Are you telling me you don't know?"

I clench my fists, feeling close to breaking point. "Don't know *what?*"

"I can't believe this," Caden mutters under his breath. "A mortal witch with immortal light magic... You have no idea the kind of power you wield. If Azriel finds out—"

"Caden." I hold up my hand, stopping him. "Please. I have no idea what you're talking about. My magic... it displays as white sometimes, but I draw on the darkness to reach it. That's one of the reasons I live so far out of the city—so there's less chance of me accidently hurting someone if it ever gets out of control."

A pulse of magic rises, unbidden, beneath my skin. Like a silent warning that I don't always have things under control. I grit my teeth, forcing the energy back down.

Caden snorts. "That burst of white light back there?" He jerks his head, indicating behind us. "That was light magic. If you learn to focus it, you could take out every demon in a ten-mile radius!"

I shake my head. That can't be true. "I... It wasn't..."

"It was," Caden counters firmly. "Trust me. I'm from the Otherworld, Sapph."

My mind reels. Suddenly, everything around me—the whir of the engine, Caden beside me in the driver's seat, the glimmer of dawn on the horizon—grows dim and indistinct. A barrage of memories floods my brain, each one sending me into a tailspin.

I'm eight years old, sitting by the ocean with Amethyst, giggling and dipping my toes in the water. If I concentrate hard, I can make the lapping waves around us glow white with light. My sister wants me to teach her how I'm doing it, but I don't know how. A storm begins to crackle over the horizon, and Amethyst tells me we have to go inside.

Fast forward. I'm fourteen, hurrying down the school hallway. I've been hiding in the bathroom for most of the lesson, but if I'm lucky, I can catch the end of it. Amethyst will kill me if I get another detention. Before I can reach my classroom, my way is barred by the three girls I've been hoping to avoid. One of them steps in front of me with her fists clenched, and white light floods the entire hall before I have a chance to stop it, sending them all flying. I run away with the word freak *ringing in my ears.*

Fast forward again. I'm nineteen and a half, dancing in a dark, sweaty club. I'm not supposed to drink yet, but I have, and the alcohol has turned my body loose and easy. When a man puts a hand around my waist and drags me into a darkened corner, I say no. He ignores me, pulling me by the wrist until no one can see us in the shadows. I don't even have a chance to scream before the whole club fills with burning, blistering white...

"Sapphire."

Caden's voice jerks me back to the present. He has pulled the car off the road and his eyes are wide with concern as he faces me. How long has it taken to drag me back from the past?

"I never..." I wipe a hand over my face, wincing at my fingertips when they come away wet. "I didn't know. No-one ever gave it a name. I thought it was just, I don't know. Random, uncontrolled magic."

There is a softness in Caden's expression that was missing earlier. I bite down on my lip, hard, to quell the sob that threatens. When he finally speaks, his voice is so gentle that my eyes flood with fresh tears.

"I'm not surprised that no-one could name it." He takes my hands in his, his thumbs stroking slow rhythmic circles on my skin. "No-one in this realm would've encountered it before. Not in a mortal. Like I said, it isn't mortal magic."

The certainty in his voice frightens me. "What you saw..."

"I know what I saw, Sapphire."

"What is this light magic, anyway?" I still feel like I'm missing something. "If it's so special, how come no-one has heard of it?"

"It's the magic of the celestials." When Caden's eyes meet mine, all the light of the Otherworld seems to glimmer within him. "Immortal power, Sapph. And it might be our shot at defeating Azriel and his army, once and for all."

15

WE DRIVE the rest of the way back in silence. My mind is reeling with the revelation.

Light magic. Celestial magic.

How is it possible that I can wield such a thing, and not even know it?

Could Caden be right? Might that be the key to defeating Azriel?

If only I knew how to control it.

He keeps glancing at me when he thinks I'm not looking. There's a strange expression on his face—almost reverent—that makes me shift uncomfortably in my seat as we grow closer to home. I still can't shake the feeling that he must have made a mistake.

Or worse, that I've somehow tricked him and created false hope that will be dashed at the first big test. With every glance, I feel more and more like an impostor.

Eventually, I can't take the looks anymore. I speak just as he pulls up in front of my cottage.

"This doesn't change anything."

He jerks his head toward me as he parks. "What do you mean? It potentially changes everything."

I shake my head. "You don't know what you saw."

He heaves a deep sigh. "Sapphire..."

"And even if you're right," I press on, determined to make my point, "I have *no idea* what I'm doing. You were there—you saw it. I have no idea how to control it! It just... happens sometimes, that's all. I don't even call it forth, like my normal witch magic. It simply bursts out when I least expect it."

Caden doesn't answer. The car idles, but to my confusion, he doesn't turn off the engine. He just pauses, fingers tapping the wheel. Then his hand clamps down on the shift stick and he throws the car into reverse.

"What are you—*whoa*!" I scrabble for the edge of my seat and hold on tight as he swings the car around in a quick U-turn. "Caden! What the heck are you doing?"

The engine roars, and I gape in the side mirror at the trail of black tire smoke we leave in our wake as the car hightails it back down the highway. Caden's expression is unreadable.

"Are you kidnapping me, or something?" I'm joking, sort-of. Something of my confusion and annoyance must finally penetrate, because he glances my way and his expression softens a fraction.

"You're right."

"I am?" *What about? Where is he taking me?*

"Your magic *is* out of control, and I sure as hell can't train you. So, I'm taking you to someone who can."

Part of me wants to order him to stop right now and take me home. I've had enough of everything in this long and horrific night, and I want to bury my head beneath my pillow and pretend the past few days haven't happened.

But the images of those poor souls being ripped apart by Azriel, their blood spraying everywhere, stays my tongue.

Instead, I take a deep breath and release it slowly, before saying, "Let's assume you asked me politely if I'd *like* to be taken to someone who can train me, and I equally politely said, yes, please, that sounds like a great idea. So, with that general courtesy out of the way, where might you be taking me, Caden?"

I'm proud of the restraint in my tone.

He has the grace to look slightly sheepish, but only for a few seconds. "We're going to the Accord Headquarters, to find the Summer Fae."

THE DRIVE—UP into the mountains, though thankfully nowhere near the scene of the slaughter—seems to stretch for an eternity.

At some point, just past sunrise, I fall into a strange half-sleep. I slip in and out of different dreams. The silver-gold light glimmering at the edge of the horizon flows into my subconscious; I dream that I'm pulling it toward me, shaping its power for myself.

The dream shifts: the sunlight grows hotter, blazing into my eyes and searing my retinas. I'm standing in the center of the light, power coursing through me, unstoppable and uncontrollable as it floods into me and out again. No beginning, and no end. Panic rises and I realize I can't hold on. This light is too strong. It will burn the entire world, and it will be all my fault.

I wake with a lurch, my eyes flying open and a gasp hovering on my lips. Bright morning light glows through the windshield—normal light, warm and cheery. I groan, unable to decide if I'd rather be asleep or awake.

"Coffee?"

I shoot a glance at Caden, who holds out a disposable cup.

"Oh, goddess, yes." I dive for the cup and sip gratefully.

The drink is lukewarm, but the caffeine is strong and exactly what I need right now.

"Thank you," I say belatedly, and he chuckles.

"I had mine about a half hour back. Stopped along the way but didn't have the heart to wake you."

"How long was I out?"

"Three hours, maybe."

I turn to study him properly. We've been in and out of this damn car most of the night and now morning. Caden has done all the driving so far, but he doesn't look fatigued in the slightest. Damn shifters.

"Want me to spell you for a bit?" At his raised eyebrows, I clarify, "Not witchy *spell*, as such. I meant, want me to drive?"

"Ah. No, I'm good."

As I take another sip of coffee, my stomach yells at me. "Don't suppose there's anything to eat in here, is there?"

He grins. "Have you ever known a shifter who *doesn't* think about food on a regular basis?"

Good point. Not that I know a lot of shifters.

As I ponder how much more attractive he is when he smiles—especially when his eyes crinkle at the corners the way they are right now—he reaches into a paper bag between the seats and hands me a snack bar.

"If you're still hungry after that, there's a bag of salted caramel popcorn in there, too."

My favorite? He got my favorite snack. "Wow. That's service. Thank you."

I ditch the snack bar and go straight for the popcorn.

"A witch with a sweet tooth and a penchant for coffee. I thought most of you were the herbal tea kind."

We are, but I don't bother answering. Instead, I stick out my tongue at him and then busy myself with eating. It's nice, this little slice of normality. Easy and warm. Right now, Caden is more relaxed than I've seen him so far, and something in me relaxes a notch, too.

I haven't forgotten what happened last night, or where we're headed now, but for a few minutes at least, I try to enjoy this unexpected moment of camaraderie.

"I must have been out for the count," I say, when I've finished eating. "I don't remember us stopping."

"Yeah." He glances at me, eyes shadowed. "Sapphire... when I got back to the car, you were..."

My heart lurches. "I was... what?"

"I don't know," Caden murmurs. "You were twitching in your sleep. You kept mumbling something, some word, over and over again. *Elebeth.* I tried to wake you, but..."

He trails off, tapping his fingers against the steering wheel. "What's Elebeth?"

Something about the word makes my skin prickle. Not with fear, but with... awareness. Like I've forgotten something very important.

"I have no idea."

It's an honest answer, but Caden doesn't look reassured.

"We're almost at the perimeter." He points through the windshield, at the road that is barely more than a gravel track now. It peters out just ahead. "I may not be able to come with you into the Headquarters. My kind are not welcome there, usually. I believe Dane may have been an exception, when he accompanied your sister."

"She told you that?"

"No. I haven't met her. Kyan mentioned it when he asked me to protect you."

"I... see." I'm not sure how I feel about leaving Caden behind, though every instinct is saying this is the right decision, coming here. "So, what happens now? How do I find the Headquarters, if I don't know where it is? I mean..."

I peer out and see nothing but forest around us, as he

slows the car and parks at the end of the road. "I have no idea where to even start looking."

Caden laughs briefly. "You won't need to. They'll find us—the Fae who guard the place. To be honest, they are likely watching us right now."

He climbs out of the car and stretches his back, and I quickly follow suit. Silence falls around us, but it isn't the silence of peace. There is a watchful air, as if we are under scrutiny by someone or something hidden, and the hairs on the back of my neck rise up.

Between one blink of my eyelids and the next, two tall, armored figures appear, standing motionless about a dozen feet away. I jerk at the shock of their appearance and take an involuntary step closer to Caden. His fingers brush against my arm, and then his hand clasps warmly around mine, our fingers interlacing.

The connection is comforting.

"Fae warriors?" I ask.

"Uh huh." Something of my nervous tension must be evident, because he adds, "You'll be fine, Sapph. The Fae will escort you, and I'll be waiting when you return."

Unexpectedly, he bends down and presses his lips to my temple. "You can do this."

Of course, I can.

My chuckle sounds almost hysterical.

I'm a witch. And a Redferne. And I'm going to find out how I can use my magic to bring down a fallen celestial.

I glance toward the stony-faced beings waiting motion-less, and take a shuddering breath in and out before walking toward them.

They nod, in unison, and turn away, not checking to see if I'm following. I'm sure they don't need to. They will be as aware of me, stumbling along behind them, as I am of them and their strange, magical presence.

A sudden wind rises, whipping through the trees and flicking strands of hair across my face. When I turn back to check on Caden, he is no longer visible.

I'm well and truly on my own, as I continue on behind the Fae, heading toward a fate even my "knowing" magic hasn't yet revealed to me.

I FOLLOW the two Fae for what seems like miles, but to be honest, is probably not that far, given I'm not a rugged, outdoor type of person. Finally, we reach a clearing where several other Fae warriors mill around what looks to be a campsite. One steps forward as I approach and recognition reduces my tension.

"Aveen?"

The warrior and his small army of Fae came to my sister's aid during the recent battle at the Aurora Spa Resort. We didn't have much to do with each other, but his presence here now provides the sense that these Fae are on the same side as me. A few minutes ago, I wasn't sure if that was the case.

"Indeed," he says. "Welcome to the Fae entrance of the Accord building, Sapphire Redferne."

"Err, thank you." I feel the need to curtsy, and only just manage to stop myself.

He gives me a traditional Fae greeting—one fist over his breastbone, clicking his heels together and nodding. I nod back, still feeling awkward, before looking around for the building he mentioned.

Only trees and undergrowth surround us, while up ahead, the track peters out into a wide, rolling field dotted with wildflowers. Not a building in sight.

Up until now, my encounters with the Summer Fae have been far and few between. They don't bother with the human world as a rule. I've always thought of them as haughty and aloof, closer to the celestials than to us mortals.

Burnished, coppery leaves twist through Aveen's reddish-brown hair, and his piercing gaze reminds me of Caden's. His eyes are pale, though, like clear ice and hard to pinpoint on actual color. Like all his companions, he is tall and clad in shiny armor.

A half-smile graces Aveen's delicate features. "I had the pleasure of bringing your sister through this entrance, not long ago."

"Amethyst told me a little about it. Thank you for your support when we needed it at the resort."

Aveen inclines his head. "She has been instrumental in spreading the word about the fallen angel. I admire her tenacity. So many of our kind will now attend the Accord Summit, thanks to her."

Yep, that sounds like Amethyst. "She has a way of achieving her aims, that's for sure."

"Quite." Aveen's lips lift into a full smile. "We owe her much. Any kin of Amethyst Redferne will find safe passage here."

Beside us, one of his warriors—a female—releases a stifled cough. Aveen's eyes dart toward her, and his mouth presses into a thin line.

"Yes. Time marches on," he says. "Come along, Sapphire. Follow me."

THE INSIDE of the Headquarters takes my breath away.

I don't know what I'd pictured—something smooth and sleek, all polished chrome and glass, I guess. But the large hall that I find myself being led across, is paneled in soft, beautifully carved wood. The light is golden and warm, and the place thrums like a living organism. With doors leading off in all different directions, and tall, graceful Fae constantly moving to and fro, I feel like I'm in a giant rabbit warren—albeit an extremely luxurious one.

Aveen leads me through one of the side doors and down a brightly lit corridor. Given the building entrance was down into the belly of the wildflower-dotted field, I can't quite figure out where all the beautiful light comes from, but I guess Fae magic and illusion are rife here, so for all I know the entrance wasn't down into a musty underground tunnel, and it was simply a mind trick to hide the true entrance.

The noise from the Great Hall dims to a low thrum as the ground beneath our feet slopes upward. We climb a short staircase to another level, and as we traverse yet another corridor, small windows cut into the side of the wall disclose that we are high in the mountains. Outside there is nothing but blue sky, sunshine, and snow-capped mountain tops in the distance.

"I don't understand the logistics of this place," I say. "Earlier, I could've sworn we were underground."

He glances back at me, looking surprised. "Logistics? It is simply Fae glamor at work, that's all."

That doesn't answer the many queries forming in my mind, but before I can say anything else, we arrive at a high, arched wooden door. An elaborate burnished knocker adorns the center of the oak, and Aveen reaches out and lifts the knocker before letting it fall. The single crashing sound reverberates everywhere, outside and within, shaking me from the roots of my hair right down to the bottoms of my feet.

When the noise dies away, a fresh wave of nerves floods over me.

Aveen steps back and starts to walk away.

I twist around, calling after him. "Wait! You're not... coming in with me?"

"I am not." Aveen's voice holds a grave note. "The celestials do not celebrate visitors. They have agreed to see you... *alone*."

In the blink of an eye, he's just... gone. Like he was never there at all.

How do they do that? It would be a damn interesting skill to learn.

When I turn back to the door, I find it ajar. Okay. That's weird. I didn't hear a thing when it opened.

Once again, I find myself on a threshold I don't wish to cross. Like last time, at Azriel's mansion, I take a deep breath and lift my chin.

Then I step forward, into the unknown, before I can change my mind.

THE ROOM IS wide and airy, with tall, floor-to-ceiling windows in the same arched design as the door. Unlike the earthy tones and feel of the lower levels, everything in this space is pale. The walls and columns dotted here and there are a cream-colored stone, and the floor is white marble, polished so highly I can see my reflection almost as clearly as if it were mirrored. White gauze drapery billow around the edges of each window, but I can't feel any breeze and none of the windows are open.

"Hello, my child."

I jump and clutch at my throat. *Who spoke? Where is... ah. There he is.*

A man walks out from behind one of the columns, his sharp features offset by long, white-blond hair, which falls past his broad shoulders. He is clothed in a white robe that shifts and moves with him as he circles me. I'm pinned to the spot, trapped under the weight of his steadfast gaze, unable even to turn with him as he paces around, studying me from every angle before coming to a halt in front of me.

"Why are you here?"

"Yes, witch. Explain your presence." A second voice joins in—this time female—and I whip around, my body finally released from whatever held it in stasis when the man studied me.

A woman has appeared, accompanied by a second man. She is equally as tall as her two male companions. All three are dressed the same, in long white robes, and all are sporting matching expressions of cool disinterest.

"I need to ask for your assistance." My voice comes out sounding tiny and pathetic in the expansive, echoing space.

"We don't consort with mortals." The second man's voice pierces through my mind. "Your insolence should be punished."

The mental assault is so sudden, I have no time to try and block it. I can't help it; I fall to my knees, pressing my hands over my ears to block out the wordless sound that resonates so loudly my head feels like it's about to explode.

I realize they are speaking mind to mind, not directly out loud like a normal human conversation. Is that what I can hear—their celestial conversation with each other? Goddess, this noise is literally mind-blowing.

They're strong—much stronger even than Azriel, and his level of power was terrifying.

Horror grips me as the first man steps forward and waves a hand toward the second one.

"Enough, Romiel."

A sense of peace and wellbeing floods through me. I slump to the floor, exhausted. I've been here less than a minute and I feel wrung out and ready to give up.

He turns to me. "We do not interfere with the dealings of mortals, child."

"Isiah, this decision to grant an audience was a mistake." Romiel shakes his head dismissively.

Isiah nods gravely. "We are above your mortal pettiness. Your squabbles can last one of your lifetimes, but that is a mere eyeblink to us."

His voice is gentle enough, but there's a finality to it that makes my chest tighten, and when all three of them turn away, I burst out, "You *can't* leave!"

Immediately, I know I've made an error, but it's too late to take back the demand.

"Please," I say in a more moderate tone. "We need you to help us. I need you."

"Do not make demands, witch," the woman says coldly. "And you may yet live."

"*But I have celestial light magic!*"

The silence that follows is deafening. Even some of the calm composure slips from Isiah's expression.

"Impossible." His eyes rake my face, and I struggle not to drop my gaze in reverence. It feels like he's peering into my soul, taking me apart, atom by atom.

"She's lying, Isiah." The heat of Romiel's glare burns through me, but I ignore him, focusing on Isiah. "She must be. This is a trick."

Isiah holds up a hand, and Romiel falls silent.

"Elebeth." Isiah turns his head, addressing the woman.

Elebeth? The name Caden said I was muttering in my sleep.

She steps forward, studying me intently, as Isiah adds, "You know what to do."

I'm not sure I like the sound of that. I breathe in sharply, readying to speak, but the two males disappear, leaving me alone with the woman.

The celestial.

Elebeth.

ONCE I'M ALONE with Elebeth, some of my misgivings fade. If I somehow already knew her name, then that means this situation is meant to be.

When I gather the courage to meet her gaze, I discover the sharp distrust and disinterest I expected to see has disappeared, leaving a hint of kindness in its place.

Some of the tension holding my muscles rigid begins to drain away.

"I've heard your name before," I say, deciding to admit to that fact without giving further detail about the dream, or the conversation with Caden that followed. I suspect mention of a hellhound would not go down well at this point. "Do we know each other?"

A soft smile graces the angel's face. "Perhaps. Time moves differently for celestials, as Isiah pointed out. You humans move from one event to the next, in a linear fashion." She waves an elegant hand. "For us, time is more... abstract."

"I see." I'm not sure that I do see, to be honest. My brain is exhausted from all that ringing and chiming in my head. At least, with only Elebeth here, she is speaking normally.

Something about her demeanor tells me that I can trust this strange being, though when she moves closer toward me, into a shaft of light that falls across the marble floor, I have to struggle not to back away or shield my eyes.

Being here is like looking into the sun; I feel as if I will leave blinded, or at the very least, irrevocably changed in some way.

"I will test your power," she says. "If you are harboring any celestial magic, it will likely be latent and instinctual. I'm afraid I will have to draw it to the surface in a way that seems... cruel."

The warning makes me shiver. "What does that involve?"

Elebeth raises one arm, holding up her hand with her palm facing me. "Threatening you."

A thunderous roar, like a tidal wave, fills the space. I open my mouth to scream, but there is no air left at all. The floor beneath my feet judders and trembles, and a giant crack splits the marble, across the middle. It opens up right where I'm standing. I jump to one side, only for a giant piece of the ceiling to dislodge and come crashing down toward my head. I push up my hands in a desperate attempt to protect myself.

And then everything turns white.

Light floods my senses, forming a molten shield around my body, blocking out the noise and the chaos around me, blinding and brilliant, and for a moment my heart soars.

There is nothing *but* the light.

When I come to my senses, I gasp, expecting to be crushed by the rubble.

But the room is intact. There are no cracks, no rubble.

Just Elebeth, gazing at me with her mouth hanging slightly open.

Somehow, I've managed to shock a celestial.

"What just happened?" I croak out. My whole body feels achy, like I've run a marathon.

Elebeth shakes her head.

"You are blessed." Her whisper reverberates around the room, settling deep inside my bones. "You have been chosen among mortals to bear the gift of the angels."

How is it possible?

"I didn't..." I swallow past the lump lodged in my throat and try again. "I didn't know."

"Clearly," Elebeth says. She is still looking at me as if I've worked a miracle. "Your power is great, but uncontrolled. You need training—from a celestial teacher—to help you refine the raw magic inside you. Right now, it's a flood, but given time, you could learn to control it."

Time? I don't have much of that left, if Azriel is to be stopped before he destroys my world.

A sound from behind has me whirling. Isiah stands watching us, his hands behind his back and a placid expression on his face. Romiel is nowhere to be seen.

"Elebeth," he says. "She spoke true?"

"She did." Elebeth casts her gaze downward, then back to me. "Isiah, this mortal child has celestial magic."

"So it seems." Isiah looks me up and down. His deep voice is polite, but something about it seems faintly familiar. Is he the one who spoke to me, back at the spa resort? "Thank you, Elebeth. You may leave us."

I glance at her standing in a ray of sunlight. Disappointment clouds her expression, but then she disappears and I wonder if I simply imagined it. My own disappointment at Elebeth's departure is intense.

I cover my anxiety with fake self-confidence.

"So, what now?" I look up at Isiah boldly, waiting for his answer. "Elebeth said I needed trai—"

"Now, you leave us." He cuts across me as if I haven't spoken at all.

My brief flurry of confidence comes screeching to an abrupt halt. "What?"

In the blink of an eye, Isiah and I are beside the arched door, which stands ajar as it did when I first entered.

"I explained earlier." He twinkles down at me, reminding me of a kindly grandfather trying to reason with a petulant child. "We don't interfere with mortal matters."

"But—"

"Thank you for confirming my curiosity." Isiah tilts his head to one side. "You have been... most enlightening."

"Please, wait!"

Before I can get out another word, I'm standing in an empty hallway. I whirl back, but the door is nowhere to be seen.

"Well, that was a big fucking waste of time. *My* time. *Human* time. Which is *precious* because we don't have much of it!"

I shout at the space where the door used to be, but nothing happens, except that my anger fizzles out and despair takes its place.

The desire to rush back to Caden and press myself into his comforting warmth grows. I have no idea where the exit is in this damn rabbit warren of an Accord headquarters, but I stride back down the corridor in the way I came, until I reach a staircase that looks familiar. Waiting at the bottom, with folded arms, is Aveen.

"Don't say anything." I hold up my hand in warning when he opens his mouth, and stomp past him, only to have to turn back. "Except to tell me how to get out of this damn place."

CADEN, thankfully, is true to his word. I find him exactly where the Fae left him, leaning against the hood of his truck with his hands in his pockets. He's staring out into the forest as I approach, seemingly a million miles away in his thoughts.

"I was beginning to wonder if they'd kidnapped you permanently." He turns his head slowly in my direction as I draw near.

Of course, he heard me approach. He's a shifter.

"I was just gearing up to stage a break-in," he adds. There is something in the depths of his eyes that tells me he is only half-joking.

"How long was I gone?" It feels like hardly any time at all. When I look at the sky, however, the sun is higher than I expect it to be.

Time. My mouth tightens as I remember the celestial arrogance.

"Long enough," he says noncommittally.

It doesn't seem like the right moment to fulfil my imagined reunion of running into his arms and being encompassed in his warmth. I'm about to turn away and climb into the passenger seat, when a contrary thought hits. *None of us know how much time we have left. Not even the celestials.*

"Caden." My cheeks heat as he lifts his gaze to mine. I swallow, but persevere despite a sudden anxiety. "Can I please hug you?"

His mouth parts as if in shock, and he straightens from leaning on the car, staring at me in silence.

I drop my gaze to my feet. "Never mind," I mutter. "It was just a silly—"

My words are cut off as he rushes forward and enfolds me in a tight embrace. I stiffen, then relax into him, wrapping my arms around his middle and releasing a sigh of relief at the comfort I find within his hold. This hug is exactly as I imagined it might be. No, it's *better* than I imagined.

We remain like that, drawing strength from one another.

It is only when his lips caress the top of my head that I finally draw back and away.

"Thank you," I say. "I needed that."

One of his brows rises, and a slight smile lifts his lips at the corners. "So did I, Sapph. It was a long wait."

WE DRIVE BACK to my cottage in relative silence. It's not uncomfortable; a few minutes in, Caden reaches over and rests a hand on my thigh. I cover his hand with one of my own, the connection keeping me grounded, even as my thoughts keep skittering back to what happened at the Accord Headquarters.

I have light magic. The impossibility still shocks me to my core, but now that the celestials themselves have confirmed it...

"I should probably let Ammie and Tee know what's been going on." There's a lot to catch up on, and for once, I know better than to push them away.

"I agree. I'll need to catch up Kyan, too, but I think it's more important you speak with your coven sisters first," Caden says.

I send a text message to Amethyst and Topaz, and part of me is unsurprised when we roll to a stop at my place and they're already waiting for us.

I sigh. "Goddess, I love them, but they are very over-bearing."

Caden snorts in a failed attempt at hiding a laugh, and I scowl at him before relenting and joining in his mirth.

"Wait till they give *you* the third degree, Caden. Then we'll see who's laughing." My chuckle rings out at his nonplussed look as I hop out of the car and hurry over to my sister and cousin.

I fling my arms around Ammie's neck and squeeze tightly, before releasing her and doing the same to Tee.

"What was that for?" Ammie says.

"It's been a rough few hours," I mumble. "C'mon, let's get inside and I'll fill you in."

She and Topaz exchange a glance before accompanying me inside. Caden stays a few paces behind, shadowing us in his usual silent way. Aside from the nod of recognition he gives Topaz, he remains expressionless.

It's only when we're inside the cottage that I notice their weary faces and the deep circles underneath their eyes.

I remember then that we've all been fighting the same battle—just from different angles. Something twists in my gut as I lower myself onto the sofa, gesturing for them to do the same. It hasn't been long since we caught up, but given everything that's happened, it might as well have been months.

I fill them in on all that has occurred in the past couple of days: meeting Azriel in his mansion, Lucia breaking into my bedroom, the stakeout at the hillside, and then our trip to the Accord Headquarters. Topaz's eyes grow wider and wider, and Amethyst's lips tighten. When I describe the horror of the blood ritual, Ammie claps a hand over her mouth.

"Sapphire!" she whispers, horrified. "How could you— what if he *saw* you?"

"He didn't," Caden says, speaking for the first time.

Everyone's heads swivel toward him.

He leans against the opposite wall with his arms folded. "I got her away, before she could sprint into the fray and try to save them all."

I glare at him. *Traitor.*

"Thank you." Amethyst's brows draw together as she spears Caden with an intent look. "For taking care of my sister."

Caden opens and closes his mouth a few times, like he doesn't know what to do with the praise.

"No problem," he mutters eventually.

"Anyway," I cut in. I can feel my cheeks heat up, and I want to move on before Amethyst can probe any further. "That's when things got really weird…"

I tell them about the blinding flash of white light that filled up the car. The way Caden recognized it immediately and took me straight to the Accord Headquarters to ask for help from the celestials—only for us to hit a dead end. When I mention Elebeth's name, Caden spears me with a look, but he doesn't interrupt.

When I finish, Amethyst releases a huge sigh.

"Hell." She leans forward, her hands on her knees, staring at me like she's never seen me before. "That explains so much."

I can tell she's thinking about all those unexplained occurrences. The time she had to pick me up from school; the letters sent home. The way other students avoided me.

And then, years later, at college, and how it had all gone horribly wrong.

Her eyes fill with tears. "Sapphire… I didn't know. I'm so sorry. I feel like I've failed you."

"No one failed me." I give her a trembling smile. "I didn't believe it myself. Not until the celestials showed me the truth this morning."

Was it only this morning? It feels like eons ago that I was there in that strange marble room.

Ammie's face hardens. "So, Aveen was right. They're exactly like all the stories… those arrogant, self-righteous pricks! God, I have half a mind to head back to the Headquarters myself! How dare they shut you out like that?"

I can't help but grin. My beautiful, fierce sister, always ready to leap to my defence at a moment's notice.

I risk a glance at Caden, who is studying both Amethyst and Topaz with interest. What is he thinking? Can he see that we all really do care about each other, even though we snipe and moan every so often?

By the soft smile playing on his lips, I suspect he sees a great deal more than I want him to.

"It wouldn't make any difference." I twist my fingers in my lap, dropping my gaze from Caden. Sooner or later, we must face reality, bleak as it is. "They made it clear they won't do anything to help us. Nothing will convince them. Right now, it looks like we're as much on our own as we've ever been." I look over to Caden again, before adding, "The witches and the hellhounds—well, some of each, at least. Off to the rescue. Against a demon horde."

TOPAZ'S long hair bounces around her shoulders as she prowls to one end of the room and back again, reminding me of a lion in a cage.

She whirls to face us. Her usual easy-going demeanor is nowhere to be seen; her eyes are wild with frustration and panic.

"We have to do something! We can't just sit around here. Amethyst, we have to tell her. She needs to know!"

I straighten at that. I thought what I'd just said about us battling demon hordes had upset her. Are they hiding something from me?

"Tell me what?"

Amethyst closes her eyes and pinches the bridge of her nose, slumping back against the couch cushions. Topaz perches on the edge of the sofa and rests her hands on her thighs. Her fingers keep clenching and unclenching.

"The Summer Fae are preparing for war," she says. "If the celestials won't sign the Accord, the Fae plan to bypass them, and take the fight directly to Azriel." Her lips press together, and her face is pale as she says, "We have three days."

My stomach drops. Three days? "That's not long enough. The Fae will be wiped out. Azriel's power is growing by the day. He'll slaughter them all like cattle. He has an army of demons and hellhounds at his disposal—not to mention half the general shifter population who have somehow succumbed to his lies."

"The shifters he hasn't killed, that is," Caden cuts in. His tone is dark, and it brings my spirits even lower.

"What can we do? How can we stop this?" I ask.

"There's nothing we can do," Ammie says.

My heart breaks at her words. I can't believe it has come to this.

"I'm so sorry." Topaz hugs her arms around her middle. "This is all my fault. If I hadn't been experimenting with my blood magic and almost died, then the Winter Fae wouldn't have used the old magic to save me. The ether wouldn't have gotten out of balance, and there wouldn't have been a rift for Azriel to get through to this realm in the first place. This is all on me."

She stands suddenly, a look in her eye I don't like. "I need to hand myself over to Luthor, or even Azriel himself, so Azriel has the soul he's been chasing. That's all there is to it. One life—mine—instead of everyone's."

"Hell, no. You can't be serious." I glare at her, as Amethyst vigorously shakes her head.

"Not happening, Tee," Ammie says.

"That is definitely *not* going to happen," Caden unexpectedly pipes up. He grins when we all look at him, slightly shocked. "For one thing, this is about far more than one human soul, when it comes to what Azriel seeks. He will never be satisfied with one life or soul. And for another thing, Kyan would kill me if anything happened to you, Topaz. Literally. And I'm not ready to die, today."

We all laugh at his attempted joke, if somewhat forlornly,

but at least the moment of humor breaks the dark despair filling the room. That is, until Ammie says, "The thing is, only another celestial has the power to match Azriel. Your magic might be a step in the right direction, Sapph, but not if it can't be controlled." She shakes her head. "I think we might be done for."

I glance around at them all, wishing desperately for a glimmer of hope in the darkness, however fragile.

"That's not quite true." A gentle voice intrudes from the corner of the room.

We all jump and turn, looking for the owner of the voice. Caden growls and leaps over the sofa to stand beside me, Amethyst springs up, clutching her throat, and Topaz peers into the shadows.

Elebeth steps forward, her hands behind her back in an imitation of Isiah. She delivers a slow smile. "Hello, Sapphire. I believe it is time to start your training."

AFTER THE SHOCK of having an actual angel in my cottage begins to subside, I introduce Elebeth to everyone and move into the kitchen to put the kettle on to boil. I don't know why, but the sense of doing something relatively normal like making tea helps with my nerves, at least a little.

Elebeth, to my surprise, accepts the cup of herbal tea I hand to her. She stares into it like she's not sure what to do, before mirroring Topaz when she takes a sip out of her own cup.

She grimaces, as if human fare is not to her liking.

"I'm afraid I don't have long." Elebeth's eyes flicker between us all. Her expression is somber. "The others don't know I'm here. I have shielded myself from their view, but I cannot maintain the shield forever."

"If you don't mind me asking..." My voice is quiet, and I cough before continuing. "Um... why *are* you here?"

"I'm here because Isiah is wrong." Elebeth places her mostly full teacup on the kitchen countertop, her pale eyes boring into mine.

Caden, who has not left my side since she appeared, stiffens. He is obviously sensitive to the proximity of a divine being.

"Because this needs to end. Because it is divine will, and I am a messenger." She bows her head. "Because you were chosen for a reason, Sapphire Redferne, to receive the gift of celestial magic, and without guidance, that gift is useless. You, and you alone, have been marked for this task and it is not up to us to question why."

A long silence follows her words. Eventually, Amethyst sets her cup down on the kitchen table where she and Topaz have seated themselves, and clears her throat.

"What are you trying to say?" She tucks a strand of hair behind her ear, staring at Elebeth. The latter looks incredibly out of place standing by the counter, as if she'd prefer to sprout wings and fly off somewhere else. "Can my sister defeat Azriel, using her light magic?"

Elebeth frowns. "That, I do not know. But I am here to offer my services. I will train her. Her powers need to be tempered, into a weapon—a blade—if you are to have any chance of stopping the fallen one. Her raw magic alone cannot be shaped in such a way, without guidance."

So, we still have a chance. That's something, at least.

"All of you must stay together, as much as you can." Elebeth glances between the three of us witches, and then turns her attention to Caden. "All of you have a part to play in what is to come. Even you, hellhound."

Finally, her eyes come to rest on me once more. "Do you accept my offer?"

The others are silent. It's my choice to make, and mine alone.

But I don't have a choice. There is no other answer I can give, except, "I do accept. When do we start?"

Pleasure ripples across Elebeth's face. "Excellent." There is a sound like the rush of bird's wings through the air; it could be my imagination, but the sunlight streaming in through the window seems to shine a little brighter. "I will return tomorrow, at sunset. Be ready."

She ripples out of existence, leaving the four of us to exhale in unison. I can't help but feel... different. Cleansed, almost.

"You're not fighting this?" I turn to Amethyst. "I'm not going to lie, I expected you to lay into her, at least a little."

She grins and shakes her head. "Lay into a celestial? No way." Her eyes soften as they study me. "Besides, it wasn't my call to make. You're an adult, now, Sapph, and it was yours, and yours alone."

I raise my brows, and then all three of us laugh madly. Caden looks confused, but then amusement tugs at the corners of his mouth, too.

I'm not alone, I realize, in that golden moment.

I never have been.

The knowledge makes the confrontation with Azriel slightly less terrifying. Only slightly, given the life-and-death stakes. But it is something to hold onto for the coming battle.

19

Caden

TOPAZ AND AMETHYST leave soon after, heading home presumably to their respective mates.

Sapphire seems quite happy when I offer to make dinner for the two of us.

"I mean, I could probably conjure something up, but I'm that weary it might not be palatable," she says. "And besides, Ammie told me Dane is a brilliant cook. Are you up to his standards, Mister Hellhound Shifter?"

Brilliant? "Hmm. I don't know about that, but I can certainly throw together an omelette and a salad."

"Sounds perfect."

While I prepare the food, Sapph heads off for a shower. A lot has happened in a short space of time and she says she needs to ground herself and get into clean, comfortable clothing. I don't blame her. I think back to the hours that she was off with the Fae. She was gone for so long, the tension roiling in my stomach grew stronger with every minute that passed. I joked to her that I was about to send out a search party, but if she hadn't gotten back when she did, I was ready to storm in there and enact a rescue.

I've never felt that way about anyone—like I needed to be with her all the time. It was the wrong decision letting her go in to the Headquarters alone.

I don't know what it is about Sapphire that attracts me most strongly. It is far more than her physical beauty. There is an inner strength and resilience that is not immediately apparent, and the more I get to know her, the more layers I keep uncovering. She intrigues me, and infuriates me, in equal measure. Here in her kitchen, whisking eggs and making her dinner feels like the most natural activity in the world.

In this moment, I do not wish to be anywhere else.

When she returns, she is wearing a long, loose skirt and a long-sleeved t-shirt with buttons down the front. We sit on the back porch to eat, on a swing seat that is the perfect size for two people. Sapphire drapes a blanket over her shoulders to ward off the evening chill and, when we're done eating, she rests her head on my shoulder and snuggles in. There is a warm tug of satisfaction in the pit of my stomach.

Her action seems natural, instinctual. Like she leaned on me without even thinking about it.

I exhale slowly and wrap an arm around her shoulders.

This isn't fake—there is no one around we need to convince. The air temperature is cool, but not freezing so we can't blame our closeness on the weather, either. Or the long day, or the alignment of the stars.

I'm here, cuddling with Sapphire, because I want to be. She is snuggled against me, because she wants to be.

After a while, she tilts her head, her gaze coming up to meet mine.

"Dinner was good, thank you."

"You're welcome." I squeeze her a little. "Are you nervous? About tomorrow night?"

I don't know what celestial light magic training entails, but nothing about it sounds easy. Sapphire shakes her head.

"The magic is already there inside me. Learning to control it can only be a good thing. I think. Besides, I trust Elebeth." She says it in that certain way of hers, her eyes bright. "She has a decent heart. I know it."

She bites her bottom lip, looking away from me. "The same way I knew about you. It was why I trusted you, even from the start. Well, that and the fact that I knew Ky wouldn't pair me with a protector who wouldn't do his job properly."

"Is that so?" Something in my chest twangs at the level of trust she seems to have in me. Her kind words—and her trust—are not deserved. She'll realize that, too, as soon as I tell her I haven't always been on the right side of good and evil. "I didn't give you much reason to trust in me. Why..."

I trail off, unsure how to finish.

Sapphire hums noncommittally. "You mean, why *do* I trust you?"

The curve of her head fits perfectly in the dip between my arm and my pec, almost as if we are made for one another.

"Yeah."

"I'm sure you had your reasons for behaving the way you did in the beginning," she says.

"You mean, like an unfeeling bastard?"

"Well, if you want to call it that."

She laughs softly, the sound reverberating through me, and I relax back into the seat, not wanting to destroy the peace between us with my ugly truth. We watch the setting sun together, streaks of pink and purple cloud cutting across the horizon, and eventually, as the light fades, I know it is time to be truly honest at last.

I sit up and put her to the side, then swivel round to face her. She frowns at me, as if she knows what I have to say won't be something she enjoys hearing. I fiddle with a stray piece of lint on my jeans, remarkably reluctant to start.

Eventually, I find the strength to begin.

"A few months back, I would have been your mortal enemy," I say. "I was one of Azriel's hellhounds, and I was his man through and through. I was a captain in his guard. I traveled here with him and his horde from the Otherworld. I believed in him, truly."

I swallow hard, wishing desperately I had a different story to tell her. I force myself to push on. "I was the perfect solider."

Sapphire seems to have shrunk into herself. Her arms are tucked around her middle, and she is frowning down at the deck beneath her feet. But I can tell she hasn't missed a word.

"What changed?" she whispers, without looking up.

"Everything changed. When we crossed the border into the human realm." I close my eyes against the flood of memories, recalling that night in minute detail. The black smoke, the scuttling of demons and other creatures in the shadows, the shock of the earth's night air on my face. I remember looking up at a sky full of stars for what I thought was the very first time, marveling at the wonder of nature, and of life. "I began to... remember things. It didn't happen all at once, but even that first night, I began to experience flashes—images, memories, things I didn't believe were real, to start with. Things Azriel had hidden from me."

Hours had turned into days, which had turned into weeks. My brain felt like someone had pushed it through a sieve; jumbled impressions and odd bursts of recollection came to me at the strangest times. Day and night blurred together; I hardly noticed the chaos unfurling around me as I realized I had been living a giant lie.

Sapphire sits quietly as I tell her everything. About how

Lucia had begun to grow suspicious of me, and how she kept lamenting that I'd changed.

But the truth is, I was returning. Coming back to myself. Waking up, for the first time in years.

"Some instinctive part of me knew that I couldn't share my inner struggle with anyone." I clench my fists on my lap. "Finally, after I don't know how long, I managed to piece together what happened. Azriel had cast an enchantment over me, many years ago. He blocked out my memories so I would do his bidding without question. I don't know why the magic wore off. Maybe it was the journey here to the human realm, setting foot on earth for the first time in years. Certainly, that was when the flashes of memory began to surface. But finally, I knew the truth. The whole truth. And it was as ugly as it gets."

I fall silent, closing my eyes. Beside me, Sapphire shifts, and then I feel her hand curve over one of my fists.

"Azriel came to earth when I was very young." I stare hard at her hand over mine. I don't dare meet her eyes; I know that if I do, I'll lose control of my emotions. "My family had rebeled against him and his kind. They traveled to earth, bought a small farmhouse, and began a new life here, intending to live in peace. My parents had me in secret, intending to raise me in the human realm where I would never be touched by the darkness. But Azriel found them. He arrived one night... and he slaughtered them. My parents, my grandparents, my aunt and uncle... everyone except me. Only, first, he told my parents before he killed them that he would spare me, and then take me back to the Otherworld to teach me how to be one of his prized soldiers and work for him to build his dark army into an unstoppable force. And he laughed as he told them there was nothing they could do to save me from my fate."

Sapphire's shock sounds in a sharp gasp. I grip her hand, lacing our fingers together before continuing.

"He did take me back there. And he did train me. And I did horrible, unspeakable things in his name. Until I arrived back here on earth, and began to remember who I really was." Finally, I meet her horrified gaze. "That's why I want to see Azriel destroyed, Sapph. He took *everything* from me... my family, my home, years of my life. My *soul*. I won't rest until he's destroyed."

"Does anyone else know?" Sapphire trails a hand down my side. Her voice shakes a little as she speaks.

"Only Kyan, and perhaps a few key members of his pack." I stare out at the darkened sky. "I caught word of his connection with Topaz. I knew his pack was one of the few hellhound packs that were considered neutral... they hadn't yet joined Azriel. When he told me about you, and your coven sisters, it gave me a glimmer of hope."

My mind goes back to that day in the forest. Sapphire, with her fierce expression, facing me down. Her dark hair falling in waves over her shoulders and down her back. Her eyes bright even in the shadows. She'd knocked the breath out of me, even back then.

"I'll do it."

Sapphire's quiet voice breaks me out of my reverie. I glance down.

"Do what?"

"I'm going to kill Azriel." Her eyes blaze.

My avenging angel. Heat surges in my chest.

"I swear to you," she adds. "He won't get the chance to hurt another living soul the way he has hurt you."

I don't know what it is. The way she's staring at me, fiery passion in her features. Our proximity, our heads turned toward each other like we're being drawn together by some magnetic force.

There's no warning. Our mouths crash together, our lips and tongues dancing in an intimate kiss that threatens to drown me in sensation. I grip her hair to hold her in place, as my other hand slides down to her waist. There's nothing gentle about this kiss; it's impatient and messy, filled with pent-up frustration and longing.

If I'm honest with myself, I've wanted her ever since I set eyes on her. Now that she's practically in my lap, crawling on top of me, I can't breathe, can't think, beyond need.

"Sapph," I groan, pulling her so close her pussy grinds into my already-hard cock. I buck beneath her, prolonging the contact, desperate for more.

"Yes." She pants somewhere near my ear, echoing my own impatience in her breaths and her husky tone. "I need you, Caden. Take me inside."

No more prompting is required. I grip beneath her thighs, pushing her skirt up and encouraging her to wrap her legs around my waist. Then I stand and carry her into the darkness of the cottage. She continues to grind against the bulge in my jeans, her tongue sliding in and out of my mouth in wordless invitation.

I groan again, helpless to stop the shudder of desire that wracks my body as I carry her into her bedroom. My movements are slower and clumsier than usual—an embarrassment for a shifter, but right now, I couldn't care less. When I place her on the bed and she falls backward, spreading her limbs, I drop to my knees and bury my head between her thighs, nipping at the bare skin exposed by her rucked-up skirt and reveling in the small, desperate sounds that escape her throat.

"*Please.*" Her scent rises around me, more delicious than anything I have ever experienced. She whimpers as I nip her again. I tug at her underwear and she shifts her hips to allow me to remove both her underwear and the skirt, then she sits up to shuck off her top before laying back again, all long pale limbs and feminine curves.

I take a moment to enjoy her exposed mound, the pussy lips swollen and ready for love. I bend my head and dip into her slit with my tongue.

She tastes like heaven, sweet and pure, and her gasp as I swipe along her seam and then return to her clit to swirl little circles around her bud sends another rush of heat straight to my already hard cock.

Hell's teeth, I want her. So bad.

She bucks beneath my mouth and I slip a finger inside her channel, then another, continuing to work her clit with my mouth while my fingers prime her body ready for my erection. I am thick and heavy and hot, and I don't know how much longer I can last without burying my flesh deep inside her.

Her hand fists into my hair to drag me up for another deep kiss. She moans, perhaps shocked at tasting her own juices on my mouth, and I push a jeans-clad leg between her thighs, giving her more hardness to buck against even as my own hips rock back and forth seemingly of their own volition.

Her skin is soft beneath my exploring fingers, and when her teeth nibble my bottom lip, a groan rips out of me. My cock twitches in my jeans, desperate for release.

It's been far too long.

She looks up at me with pleading eyes, an enticing mix of innocence and wanton invitation. She scrabbles at the front of my jeans, stroking the length of my erection in maddening, slow movements. *Teasing.*

Then, she takes control, ripping at my clothing, trying with shaking hands to undress me. I take a moment to pull away from her and quickly undress, then I'm back over her on the bed, our naked skin touching at last, all the way from shoulders to toes.

"No. Roll over," she says, her voice husky, and she pushes at my shoulders and chest to urge me to roll onto my back. In one slick movement, she lifts her leg and sits astride me, her arms braced each side of my head and my erection poking out from between her legs as she pushes her mound against my balls.

I stare up at her in a daze. "You don't know what you do to me, Sapph."

The admission trips from my tongue before I can stop it. I can't help it; when I'm around her, I feel like I'm not in the driver's seat anymore.

She angles her hips forward, stroking up and down my ready flesh until I grunt with frustration and grab at her hips to hold her steady.

"I think I might know," she whispers, and her seductive smile almost undoes my control altogether.

"I can't wait, beautiful woman. Beautiful witch. Do you want this?"

Her hair falls everywhere, mussed and sexy, and her cheeks are flushed. The way her lips are slightly parted as she runs her fingers over my chest is incredibly sexy.

The slick wetness from her pussy that now coats my cock is answer enough.

When she says in a coy yet teasing tone, "I've wanted this ever since I first laid eyes on you," I know there is no turning back.

I grab her and roll us over, pinning her to the mattress and covering her with my body. She shivers from head to toe. I settle my hips between her open thighs, allowing the head of my organ to rest at her channel entrance, and tease her nipples, first one then the other, enjoying the little cries and moans that erupt out of her.

"I could take you apart, just like this." I lower my mouth to her shoulder, letting my words brush along her skin, before

I nip at the soft point between collar bone and neck. "Without even entering you," I add, and nip her again.

She gasps and arches into me. "Don't you dare leave it like that."

I grin, my shifter rising as it recognizes its mate, and then I can't tell who moves first, but I'm finally inside her.

"Oh, goddess, Caden, that feel so... good..."

She moans as I thrust, deepening the connection, enjoying her slick heat around me. Her legs wrap around my hips and her arms pull me close, and I give in to the urge and fuck her, hard and fast.

Her first orgasm hits, and she stares straight into my eyes as I continue to thrust my hips, riding her through it. Her pussy undulates around me, coaxing my own orgasm which is only seconds away.

Then she climaxes again, the shock on her face an aphrodisiac beyond anything I could ever imagine.

Her mouth opens, her eyes widen, and her head tilts back as her whole body begins to rock and shudder with the force of her release. Her inner muscles clamp down hard on my cock, sending me over the edge into a strong orgasm of my own.

I spill deep inside her with a growl, collapsing on top of her, then roll to the side so I won't crush her, feeling the last flutters of her orgasm eventually subside along with my own.

We just lie there, still physically connected, catching our breath. My body feels like Jell-O, boneless and wobbly. Then she moves, breaking the connection, and curls into my side, her breath huffing gently against my chest. I slide my arm beneath her and pull her close.

Part of me is afraid of this—about how she'll react, after the fact, so to speak. Particularly if she didn't have the chance to properly digest what I told her before we gave in and sated our desire.

Will she think me impulsive? Will she assume that what we just did was an irrational urge, satisfied under deadly circumstances, and nothing more?

My own feelings for her are... complicated, to say the least.

I listen to her breath as it deepens and evens out. She falls asleep slowly, inexorably.

I should probably get some sleep myself, while I can. I don't need much. Just a couple of hours...

The battle between dark and light, good and evil, rages on somewhere, no doubt. But for tonight at least, Sapphire is here in my arms, and we are safe in this warm cocoon. Hidden from the world. Together.

I slide into sleep, my dreams populated by the ravages of war and death. The images that play out during slumber are a stark reminder that, even in moments of relative safety, danger lurks close by.

Sapphire

I WAKE COCOONED in Caden's embrace, his warmth spreading through me and his latent strength wrapped around me. I can't imagine anywhere else I'd rather be.

Is this what Ammie and Tee feel, when they're wrapped in their respective lovers' arms? If so, no wonder they've both been walking around with massive smiles on their faces.

When Caden realizes I'm awake, he trails his long fingers up and down my side until I lose my breath.

We fall into each other once again. Holding him like this feels as easy as breathing. For a few precious hours, I'm consumed with his touch. Nothing else exists beyond this room, beyond *us*. The bed becomes our own little world. Only the sunlight that travels over the floor, casting long shadows by mid-afternoon, alerts us both to the passage of time.

And finally, the real world comes knocking once more.

Elebeth arrives for my first training session.

"AGAIN, Sapphire. That was not good enough."

I glance up at the angel from my kneeling position on the ground. We are outside my cottage, in the back garden, and the grass is soft beneath my knees. I'm panting heavily and damp with perspiration. Practising fighting using light magic is exhausting and I am beginning to wonder if I have what it takes to use my light magic as a deliberate weapon against Azriel and his horde.

"I know, but I need to take a break," I mumble. We've been at the training for hours, and I'm totally spent.

Elebeth just stares down at me, with one brow raised. Her arms are folded across her chest and her expression holds no emotion, bar disdain. A shiver runs down my spine when I meet her stare.

This isn't a shifter or a Fae. This is a celestial—a creature who doesn't abide by the rules of the human realm. She may look like one of us, when she wishes to show us a human façade, but she is something else entirely and I have to remember not to take her presence for granted.

I grit my teeth and struggle to my feet.

"All right." I rub a hand over my face. "Just give me a minute. Please?"

"Sapphire." Elebeth's face is like stone. "There is no time. You must continue now."

"One minute. It's nothing to you, surely?" I stumble over to the porch steps, where I've left a drink bottle, and take a swig of water, trying to quell the trembling in my hands.

As I walk back to the center of the garden, Elebeth waits with her hands raised. I heave a sigh and mirror her stance, ignoring the ache in my wrists.

We decided against practising inside, for fear of destroying my home.

After a brief argument earlier, Caden agreed to take a long walk while I begin my training. He was stubborn, but when

Elebeth told him that his presence could endanger my concentration, he finally conceded and disappeared.

I have no doubt he will be back the second we finish. I'm sure he is lurking nearby. And for some reason, that thought comforts me.

I screw my eyes shut as Elebeth sends another wave of magic in my direction. This is the seventh attack wave I've dealt with in the past hour, hence my exhaustion. This time, her magic takes the form of a hundred winged creatures that descend on me from above, knocking me to the ground. Their sharp talons pierce my skin and I cry out, twisting and thrashing and wondering when this latest torture will end.

"Concentrate!" Elebeth shouts above the din.

I am. Or at least, I'm trying.

I clench my fists and loosen them, sending a wave of white light flooding through the space. My soul feels like it is splitting in two. I can barely hold on. My eyes burn with the force of my efforts, and I gasp out something unintelligible before slumping forward.

"I can't," I moan. "Elebeth... I can't. I can't."

"You *must*."

To my surprise, she presses a hand to my shoulder before gliding away. The surface of my skin tingles at her touch, and I realize she must have sent a pulse of healing energy through me.

When I rise for what feels like the millionth time today, Elebeth's eyes are soft.

"We shall try for one more hour." She tilts her head, as if assessing my ability to continue. "You are doing well, child. Your magic is there. But you must do better. Strengthen it. Control it."

It hits me then. It wasn't Isiah who spoke to me that day at the resort; it was Elebeth.

"You! It was *your* voice I heard, encouraging me..."

"Of course." She smiles gently. "And now we hone your skills. One more hour, and then you rest. Tomorrow will be the real test."

"Oh?" I grimace. *I don't like the sound of that one bit.* "How so?"

"I will unleash the full force of my power," Elebeth replies, before she raises her hands once again. "And then, we shall see if you are truly ready."

CADEN RETURNS the second we finish for the day. There is no question of him heading home to his own place. I don't even need to ask him to stay; he simply folds me into his arms and tells me to shower and climb into bed, and then he delivers dinner on a tray. The comfort of having him wrapped around me during the night is tempered by the crushing reminder of what tomorrow will bring. My sleep is restless, broken with strange dreams. A nightmare leaves me gasping for breath—I dream of Isiah discovering Elebeth training me and dragging her away, and then of being left to face Azriel alone with no idea what I'm doing.

Nightmares aside, Elebeth returns as promised the following day. By the time mid-afternoon rolls around, a shred of impatience has begun to crack through her serene façade.

"You won't focus." She glares at me.

"I'm trying." I glare back, just for a moment, then drop my eyes from the cold annoyance in hers.

"You are not trying hard enough." She flexes her fingers. "You have the power to level an army of demons, and still, you hold back. Your magic fails you. No. Actually, *you* are failing your magic."

Ouch! That is never something a witch wishes to hear.

"It's easy for you to say." I hope my voice doesn't sound as whiny to her as it does to my own ear. "You've had literally forever to master this whole celestial magic thing. I have *three days.*"

"One and a half days," Elebeth corrects, tilting her head toward the window, as if to indicate the setting sun. "Although technically, you have had this magic forever, so you have had your whole lifetime to master it. You just... didn't."

"Thanks," I grumble. "That makes me feel so much better."

"So preoccupied with *feelings.*" The angel draws close, assuming what I have come to dub the "celestial battle stance", with feet equal distance apart, hands by her sides, and a look of readiness in her expression. She tosses her hair back over her shoulders. "How very human."

I roll my eyes at her just as she throws a lightning bolt my way. I block it with magic—a huge blast of white heat that disappears almost as quickly as it arrived.

"Good," she says. "At last you show some control. Now, repeat."

And with that, we're off again.

By the end of the day, I think I hate Elebeth. I know she must hate me.

Her expression is set in stone.

I straighten for the final time, growing cold as I peer in her direction. Has she had enough? Is she about to smite me where I stand, out of sheer frustration?

"So." I force my tone to remain light, even as my chest constricts. "What time tomorrow?"

Her gaze snaps to mine. Her eyes are like shards of ice; I can't help but shiver. "Our training is at an end."

"But..."

"I can teach you no more," Elebeth murmurs. "My superiors have grown... suspicious. They have begun to question my recent disappearances. I cannot afford to visit you again, young witch."

My chest tightens with panic. As frustrating as the sparring sessions are, as merciless a teacher as Elebeth can be, without her, I'm lost. I don't know how to draw forth my light magic at whim, and I certainly don't know how to wield it to full effect against an enemy.

She moves toward me as if she can read my thoughts, and her expression turns fond.

"You have the ability, Sapphire. You must continue alone. Remember: the strength is inside you. It is there already. Do not be afraid of it. The light magic is a natural part of you."

Her palm rests on my temple, and my eyes flutter closed.

When I open them again, she is gone.

ON THE MORNING of the third day, I have to force myself out of bed.

I'm completely drained of energy. With no Elebeth to guide me, I don't have any idea how to invoke the light magic at will. Caden has faith in me, but I can't help my skepticism.

"It isn't something I can turn on and off like a tap," I grumble, pressing a kiss into his bare shoulder as he lays there with his hands behind his head. I gather up clothing ready to head into the bathroom, part of me enjoying his unabashed gaze on my naked form.

"I think I need... I don't know. Some kind of threat."

"I can be very threatening." He obligingly growls, grabbing my arm as I wander past and bringing my wrist to his mouth. He allows his teeth to scrape along the surface of my inner wrist. His breath flutters on my skin and instead of feeling threatened, I giggle. I push him away.

"You're impossible."

He sits up. The bedcover pools around his hips and I suppress a sigh of longing.

He eyes me with a faint frown. "Would it help if I was in hellhound form?"

A spark of interest catches me; I've never seen his shifter form before. I tilt my head, looking him up and down. "Maybe. I don't know. Are you a threatening hellhound, or the cute puppy type?"

Another growl erupts and he lunges for me, throwing me onto the bed and pinning me down with one thick arm either side of my head. "Want to find out?"

So that's how I end up back in the living room, sparring with a hellhound.

Caden is no cute puppy, that's for sure.

As a hellhound, he is huge, his shoulders too wide to fit through my bedroom door. His paws are bigger than the dinner plates we ate from last night. His head sits just beneath the light fitting hanging from the ceiling, and I circle him with trepidation, my heart pounding.

It's Caden, I keep telling myself, over and over. *He won't hurt me. He... cares for me.*

The hellhound lowers his head as I swivel to face him. His eyes glitter a strange crimson that has taken over the delicious green of the gaze I can't get enough of. There are traces of old scars criss-crossing his muzzle. He stares at me, watchful and still, waiting for me to make the first move.

"Caden, if this is going to work, I need to feel *threatened*. Not *safe*, with you."

He tilts its head and then his upper lip curls, displaying massive teeth, each one larger than my forefinger. Each one sharp enough to cut easily through flesh and bone.

Caden disappears from the hellhound's gaze and only Azriel's captain of the guard is left in its place.

A growl fills the room. Not a playful growl, like earlier, but a full-on throaty growl that holds menace and death in its cadence. The faint smell of smoke reaches my nostrils, and for the first time since we started our sparring, fear ripples through me.

Magic rises in response, the power thrumming just beneath my skin. When I look down at my palms, they glow silver-white.

I curl my fingers over my traces of magic, holding it ready, just in case.

Then I look up at Caden, nodding solemnly.

Keep doing that, hellhound, and this is going to work out just fine.

By evening, both of us have had more than enough.

Caden is back in human form, and we collapse on the sofa, chests heaving and sweat turning our faces shiny.

One advantage of a hellhound shift that I hadn't really processed till now, is that when he shifts back, he is naked. I can't say that I disagree with that development, though he throws on a zip-up hoodie and track pants that he asked me to fetch from his truck.

His head tips toward me and he rolls his shoulders a few times, huffing a laugh. "Jeez, you pack one hell of a punch, Sapph."

I wrinkle my nose and lean in, giving him a peck on the lips. "Sorry."

"Don't be." He smiles lazily. "That was amazing. Every time you hit me with that light magic, it felt like I was either about to die of the rapture, or ascend to a heavenly place. Or both."

"Is that... um... good?"

"Hell yeah. Being bathed in celestial magic is both dangerous and delightful. The problem for your enemies is that they won't know the difference between the two, until it is too late for them. At least with me, you stopped before you could do any damage. I trusted you to do that, just as you trusted me to threaten without actually going too far."

Before I can respond, the door buzzes. I hop off the sofa to answer it, my whole body aching with tiredness.

Topaz and Amethyst pile into the cottage, followed, to my surprise, by Kyan and Dane. I greet them all happily enough once I've got over my shock, and introduce Dane and Caden, who haven't yet met.

"It's good to see you." Kyan pulls me into a brief hug, ruffling my hair.

Dane merely nods, and I return his faint smile with a wide one of my own.

"Topaz tells me you've been busy." Kyan's eyes drift toward Caden.

Heat rises in my cheeks and I shrug, not quite meeting Kyan's gaze.

"You know how it is." I keep my tone firmly neutral. At least, I think I do. "End of the world and all that."

Kyan chuckles broadly, clapping me on the back before moving off to talk to Caden.

"So." I join Amethyst and Topaz who are standing by the fireplace staring between me and Caden. I hold up a hand. "Don't say it."

Topaz's brows rise, but Ammie gives a small snort. "Wouldn't dream of it, sis."

Dane silently settles in the armchair opposite Caden and Ky, watching everyone with interest.

"What's the occasion?" I ask, hoping they won't confirm what I think they're about to say. There's likely only one reason to gather like this; one eventuality that we've all been desperately wanting to avoid.

Amethyst lays a hand on my arm, squeezing briefly. "It's happened."

I close my eyes, like I can somehow block out the news if I try hard enough. But I can't. Not this time.

"What's happened?" I need her to say it; admit it out loud.

Ammie takes a deep breath and releases it in a rush. "The Fae have declared war on Azriel."

21

THERE'S no time to lose.

Topaz, Amethyst, and Dane pile into Kyan's truck, parked on the road outside my cottage. I'm about to follow them, but Caden lays a hand on my arm, stopping me in my tracks.

"Want a ride?" He cocks a grin at me, holding out a motorcycle helmet.

I gape at him before I splutter out a laugh, my shoulders shaking. "Sure. Why not? Only..."

I wave a hand, muttering a simple incantation, and we are both suddenly clad in appropriate wear for a motorbike ride —leathers, jeans, and boots.

"Ah." He looks down at himself, then back up at me. "Thanks. I think."

"You're welcome." I give him a smirk, and take the helmet out of his hands. "Let's go."

We follow behind Ky's truck, which heads down the highway. Despite everything—the impending sense that this is our last shot at stopping Azriel; our moment of truth—I can't prevent the exhilaration singing through my veins. The ride feels like it did before—the taste of freedom on the wind.

Only this time, when I wrap my arms tightly around Caden, I feel so much more connected to him than that first ride.

A thick cloud of dust covers the horizon. It looks like a storm is coming our way. But as we get closer to the epicenter of the battle, on the plain in front of the mountain range where Azriel killed all those shifters, I realize nothing in nature could come close to this unnatural event. The air is thick with magic. More Fae than I've ever seen before dart through the sky, bristling with defensive spells, wrestling with snarling demons, snapping hellhounds, and hideous beasts whose names I don't even know.

Screams and yells fill the air, and the smell of death is already upon us, even before we reach the edge of the battleground.

Hellhounds patrol the perimeter. They are fewer in number than I expect—some no doubt killed at the blood ritual, and others by us in earlier battles at the beach and the resort—but there are enough remaining to pick off any of the flying Fae that fall to the ground in defeat. The hounds finish off what the demons start with bloodthirsty relish, tearing into the flesh of anyone they can reach. The carnage all around us turns my stomach, and I screw my eyes shut, clinging tightly to Caden and praying for the strength to get through this

Please, goddess, let us live. Let us survive this, and destroy the evil before it can take hold any more.

I sense Azriel in the distance before I see him, the draw of his dark power a strange pull on my senses. He stands on a rise above the battle, a black blot on the landscape. He's like a poisonous shadow, spreading his evil miasma over everything, turning the whole landscape pitch black and rotten, just like I imagine the Otherworld to be.

If we let him win, then even the sun will fall to the night.
Everything will die.

The motorbike rumbles to a halt. I slide off the back, tugging off my helmet and hurrying with Caden over to where Ammie, Tee, and their protector men are waiting.

We've entered the eye of the storm, or at least, it feels that way. All around us, a magical battle is raging. Caden grabs my arms and pulls me to one side just before a Fae warrior, fully bedecked in silver armor, hurtles to earth from above with a massive *thud*.

Before we can do anything, he staggers to his feet with a wild look in his eyes. His glassy gaze slides over us without recognition, but something in him must recognize us as friend, not foe. He touches a shaking hand to his forehead, where blood drips from his tangled curls. He staggers back into the fray before we can stop him and is soon lost in the whirlwind of dust and bodies and creeping darkness.

Topaz and Ammie are affected by the overflow of magic in the atmosphere; their eyes glimmer and their hair flies outward in all directions, as if charged with electricity.

The same thing is happening to me. I shake my head, trying to flick back the wayward locks of hair out of my face, but to no avail. My body hums, the darkness inside me rises, and now that I'm aware of it, I feel the light magic rise up, equally powerful.

I am both light and dark, and I don't know how long I can hold everything contained.

Caden touches my shoulder. "Take deep slow breaths, Sapph. You've got this. I believe in you."

I meet his steady gaze, gulping in air. "Okay. I can do this. I can."

I take in the battle around us, wondering how it will end. I turn back to Caden. "Whatever happens, know that I'm glad to have met you. I believe in you, too, Caden. I... care."

Shock registers in his eyes, and then a grin transforms his face from severe to sexy. Even here, he has the ability to make an impact on my emotions. "I care too, Sapph. And when this is done, I'll show you how much."

"It's a deal," I murmur, and turn away to face whatever the future is about to bring.

"There's too many of them." Topaz's voice is frantic, and Ammie nods wildly.

Sure enough, when I follow the line of her gaze, I realize she's right. The bright glints of Fae armor are few and far between across the battlefield; one Fae can easily take on two or more demons, but there are so many of the latter, more and more pouring forward from some hidden place, as soon as one of them falls.

The Fae are becoming overwhelmed.

Kyan and Dane shift and bound ahead, snapping and snarling as they gallop into the fray. Then my sister and cousin step forward, shooting magic in every direction, and I know they won't stop until we win. Or until they die.

I will not let that happen.

I am not going with them. I have my own destiny, my own place in this battle. My heart clenches as I realize this might be our final goodbye.

Ammie looks back, staring hard at Caden.

"Protect her. Love her. Whatever happens," she calls out.

Caden nods. "I will. I do. I promise."

I do? He loves me?

Focus on that later.

If there is a later.

I return my gaze to the one who started it all. Azriel.

The fallen angel stands still, presiding over the bloodshed and destruction as if watching a lightly entertaining TV show. Nausea roils in my stomach as I see he isn't standing on an earthy rise as I thought. Instead, he stands atop a mountain of fallen Fae bodies. Somehow, he has drawn the bodies to him, and then climbed to the top, as if wanting to impart a final message of indignity and disrespect to the departed.

Rage fills me and I clench my fists, feeling the heat of my magic sitting right there at the surface of my skin, ready to explode.

Caden watches me.

"Your move, Sapph," he says. "Wherever you go, I will follow. I have your back."

A wave of determination runs through me. Too many have died already. With every second that passes, more die, and soon, it could be the ones I love that are obliterated by the evil piece of crap standing on top of those bodies.

"It's time," I say.

I fight my way forward, toward Azriel, blasting those in my path with magic to toss them back and out of the way.

As we get closer, my fears begin to grow. Elebeth's doubtful expression on the last night we trained together haunts me.

Am I good enough? Strong enough? Who am I to think I can go up against a celestial of any kind, fallen or not, and live?

"Concentrate on your light magic." Caden's voice in my ear spurs me on. I grit my teeth and keep going.

A demon wraith steps into my path, its blackened razor-sharp teeth flashing as it grins at me. A blur of movement too fast to catch rushes past me and then Caden's huge hands rip the wraith's head right off its shoulders. I blast the corpse with a shot of magic for good measure, and it disintegrates into ash.

We forge ahead, dodging flying bodies and blasts of magic, jumping aside as a hellhound's giant maw snaps shut mere inches from where I was standing moments earlier.

My hands are already shaking from adrenaline and terror. I have no idea if I am going to be up to the task ahead. It makes no sense for me to have the magic of the immortals. I'm an ordinary witch, even though my mother was an incredibly powerful witch, as was my aunt.

Maybe the power *was* a divine gift, like Elebeth suggested. A sign from above; a call to a higher purpose. But I don't feel like a chosen one. Far from it. Right now, I'm more scared than I've ever been in my life, and the closer we get to Azriel, the smaller and less powerful I feel.

I glimpse a familiar face in among the wounded masses. Avreen, slumped against a pile of rubble, lies motionless. A thin line of blood trickles from his parted lips.

Oh, no. Is he dead? Where do Fae go when they die? What happens to them?

We're at the center of the battle now. Howls of fury and bright currents of magic race through the air around us, forcing us to duck behind the dead body of a particularly giant hellhound. My stomach turns as I stare into one of its glassy eyes. In death, it seems less frightening.

Death, the great leveler.

Except when it comes to the celestials.

Caden braces a hand against my shoulder. "Sapphire... this is as close as we're going to get."

I'm frozen to the spot. Only his touch keeps me sane.

"I don't think I can do this." My voice shakes. "I don't know what I'm doing. I can't control my magic. I haven't trained enough. Elebeth said..."

"Hey." Caden squeezes my shoulder and tilts up my chin, forcing me to look into his eyes and ignore the maiming and killing going on around us. "Forget Elebeth. Forget all of them. Fuck, if I could take your place, I would do it in a heartbeat. You know that, right?"

My eyes fill with tears. "Caden..."

"You're so much stronger than you know." He presses a

kiss to my forehead. His fingers slide through my hair, a small, soft gesture in such harsh surroundings.

I take comfort from his touch, but in the end, this task is on me. No one else. I suck in deep breaths, trying to control my panic. "Okay." It's time to be a grown-up. "I *have* to try."

With that, I turn away. There's nowhere to run, nowhere to hide. Nobody can do this for me anymore.

I have to attempt the rest alone.

22

Azriel hasn't seen me yet. His gaze is cast toward the skies, where the Fae and demons are locked in combat. He scans the heavens like he's searching for something.

What is he waiting for?

I push the thought away, letting my power begin to surface. It rises up, filling my hands, my arms, my whole body with hot, burning light. When I hold out my hands in front of me, the light pools between my palms, glowing and heating my skin, becoming brighter and brighter until I can barely even look at myself.

I push on, through the last few feet toward the mountain of the dead. As I do so, some of the demons and wraiths begin to notice the light pulsing in my hands. Out of the corner of my eye, I see some of them shrink away. A couple of wraiths bare their teeth at me, black gums peeled back. I flick my wrist, barely looking at them; a bolt of white light shoots out from my palm and that's all it takes to evaporate them on the spot.

I have no idea what I look like when I reach the base of

the mound. There is so much white light, so much glare, that it is hard to see anything at all.

But, through the glare, I make out Azriel. He stares down at me, his mouth open and his black eyes wide. Whatever he was waiting for, it wasn't me.

His astonished face sends a faint ripple of satisfaction through me, cutting into the terror.

That's right, you bastard. I'm the one with the power now.

He's tiny, a faint spot in the light that pours through my body, spilling out all over the battlefield, where everyone and everything is coming to a halt. Everyone gapes at me, a powerhouse of white. I don't even feel like me anymore. I have a *star* inside me. A supernova. Immense, immeasurable power: the power of the gods. The power to create, and the power to destroy.

Wield it wisely. Words rush through my head, making perfect sense, and yet, making no sense at all.

"You are nothing." My voice doesn't sound like mine. It isn't mine. And yet, it is.

Is this what it feels like, to finally know your power?

"No!" Azriel's scream cuts into my semi-conscious state. "This world is mine! I will not be defeated. You cannot destroy me! I am *immortal!*"

So am I.

The power rages through my mind, through my body. Through every cell that makes up who I am. The overwhelming force of the universe is at my disposal, and suddenly, I *know* that he is the weaker of the two of us.

I open my mouth, and more light pours out of it, wave upon wave, consuming everything in its path. But I have control. I direct all of it toward Azriel. "You are nothing."

"The celestials *will* bow before me when they see what I've achieved!" Azriel howls. "What I will create! This world is my destiny!"

"Your destiny lies in ashes. Your destiny lies where you sprung from." The voice coming out of me seems to reverberate through the very earth beneath our feet. "I see your true form, Azriel."

I hold up a hand, slow and steady. The light burns through my skin, tearing it apart from the inside. Somewhere, buried deep, my mind is screaming for me to stop. *It's too much, too intense. He'll burn away... but so will I...*

I can't let go. I can see *everything*. Every strand of fate, woven together to create this moment. I know exactly what I have to say.

"*I annihilate you*," I whisper.

A scream shreds through the air, and Azriel crumples to the ground.

And then everything goes black.

Caden

THE WARRIORS around me have fallen silent. They're as transfixed as I am by the light that flows like a river from the slim female figure standing below their leader.

My breath catches in my throat as Sapphire raises her hands. She's radiant with white light, her eyes lit up like a furnace. For one brief, terrifying moment, she looks like an angel—a celestial, come to wreak vengeance on the world.

And then Azriel begins to scream.

I race toward Sapphire. Most of the onlookers have turned their faces away, blinded by the light. I hold up a hand to my shield my eyes, grit my teeth, and press on.

I don't care; I'll go blind if I have to. I just need to get to her.

I lower my hand just in time to see Azriel crumble into dust before my eyes. The force of power that surges from

Sapphire knocks me back, onto my ass. I jump to my feet and rush forward, pushing against the stream of light as if I'm wading through a raging current. I place one foot in front of the other, over and over, one tiny step at a time.

She needs me. I have to reach her.

All around me, demons are shrinking into nothingness, being drawn back to whatever Otherworldly hell they came from, without Azriel to hold them here. Hellhounds whine and whimper, loping backwards in obvious desperation. I ignore them all and continue forward. My skin burns. My eyes will likely never recover. But I have to get to her.

"Sapphire!" I shout, over the howl of the wind and the storm of light everywhere. "It's over! You can stop now!"

She doesn't respond. Instead, a column of pure light continues to pour out of her, all around and up toward the heavens.

I curse and lunge, grabbing at her wrists. The heat sears my skin and I smell burnt flesh.

Hers? Mine?

"Sapphire." I wrench at her, shaking her by the arms. "If you don't let it go, you'll *burn*. We'll all burn. Please... let go, my love. My brave beautiful love. You can let go. You have control of it, remember?"

She sobs, and her hands slide up to grab my forearms.

The pain is unimaginable, hotter than anything I've ever felt, and I've lived in the Otherworld. This feels like molten metal poured over my skin. But I don't let go; we sway together, holding onto each other in the eye of the storm of light.

"I've got you!" I shout hoarsely. Some of the light in her eyes fades away, and for a second, her terrified gaze locks onto mine. "Let it go!"

Her eyes roll back in her head and flutter closed. The light and the heat abruptly cut off and she sags into my arms. I catch her before she can sink to the ground, staggering backward, slipping on bits of dead body beneath my feet. Then I swing her up into my arms, and get a firmer grip on my balance. All around us, the remaining light begins to flow away. Not back into Sapphire, as I thought it would, but up and away, eventually disappearing into the ether.

THE BATTLEGROUND IS A MESS. Bodies lie everywhere. Many Fae are dead, though some are merely wounded. In the distance, I catch a glimpse of two dark, hulking shapes that might be Kyan and Dane, alongside two smaller female figures with flowing dark hair.

Topaz and Amethyst. They survived.

Azriel is nowhere to be seen. Neither are any of the demons, nor the hellhounds who had been fighting alongside them.

Everything is silent, except for faint pleading cries of the wounded breaking through the eerie stillness.

Sapphire lies motionless in my arms. For a sickening moment, I think she might be dead. She's pale enough. But when I press two fingers to her neck and lean in close, I feel a faint pulse, and her breath brushes against my cheek in a steady rhythm.

A wave of relief crashes over me, and I bow my head over her body, sending a silent prayer of thanks to anyone who might be listening.

"I didn't think you were going to stop," I mumble, even though I know she can't hear me. I stroke a lock of hair off her cheek, settling it into place behind her ear. "You had me worried for a second, there."

Her slack hand brushes against the skin of my forearm,

and I flinch. There are two identical burn marks branded into my flesh from where her palms touched me.

"Thanks for those, by the way." I smile down at her. "When they heal, I reckon they'll leave pretty badass-looking scars."

Now that I've started talking, I don't seem able to stop. I don't know why, but it's easier to get the words out like this, when she's here but not listening. I can tell her all the stuff I want to say, but... it's safer, this way.

"The thing is," I continue, my voice rough, "before you, I had no-one. Not a soul. And... I didn't want to let you in. I guess I was worried about what might happen if I did. But I'm not worried any more, Sapphire, I'm not. 'Cause you're the best thing that's ever happened to me, and that will never change."

I dip my head low, brushing my lips against her temple. "I love you."

I hold her like that for a long moment, breathing in tandem with her, until she releases a soft sigh.

When I draw back, her eyes are open, though her expression is dazed.

"Hey." My heart pounds. "How do you feel?"

She blinks up at me. She looks hazy, barely hanging onto consciousness. "Like I've been struck by lightning."

I grimace at her. "That good, huh?"

She gives me a slow nod. One of her fingers comes up slowly to caress the side of my face. I want to tell her to save her strength, but I don't have the heart for it. Not when she's touching me like this, so gentle. The blistering heat has gone; her touch is cool and soothing.

"By the way," she murmurs. "I love you, too."

I catch my breath. "You heard?"

"I did."

I lean down and kiss her, lightly.

When I pull back her, she shifters her eyes left and right. "What happened? Is Azriel..."

"Gone. Obliterated. Or at least, as much as a celestial can be. He's gone from this world, that's for sure. Thanks to you, Sapph."

"He's really gone. For good?"

I chuckle. "You turned him to ash, honey. I'd say its pretty much for good."

Her exhaled sigh is breathy, like she doesn't quite have the energy to celebrate the good news.

"The demons are back in the Otherworld, where they belong," I add. "Everyone in this world that Azriel held under his power will now be free."

"Like your pack members?"

"Yes. Like them. Like me. You saved everyone, Sapph."

"No." To my surprise, she shakes her head. "Not everyone."

"Oh?"

She leans against my chest, tilting her head up to face me. Her eyes are shining. "*You* saved *me*."

"Always will," I say.

23

Sapphire

"THIS IS IMPORTANT. Essential. Sapphire, this is the most important thing you will *ever* do. So please, *please*. Take this seriously!"

My sister's eyebrows pinch together in her familiar, intense way as she glares down at me. I stare up at her from the end of my bed, unmoved.

"I just don't see why it's such a big deal." I gesture between the two dresses she's holding and shake my head. "They're both nice."

Amethyst huffs with defeat and rolls her eyes. I giggle at her dramatics, for once not bothered by them. She holds up the dress on the left.

"Blue..." She holds up the other one. "Or green?"

I look at her helplessly. "Green?"

Her eyes narrow. "Are you just saying that to get me off your back, or do you actually like it better?"

"Um... I like them both."

"I despair." Amethyst whirls and hangs up the blue dress

in the closet, before forcing me to my feet so she can hold the other one up to my body. "Sapphire, you're receiving the *highest honor* in the supernatural world. The Fae Chains of Aother! Everyone is going to be there at the Accord dinner today! Shifters, banshees, Fae... even the celestials, for goddess' sake! You have to look the part."

She stands behind me as we gaze into the mirror together. "So... does this dress convey that message?"

I snort. "I don't think any article of clothing can say all that." To mollify her, I take the dress out of her hands and smile before ushering her away. "Now let me get dressed. I'm all grown up now, remember?"

She gapes at me, then we both break into laughter.

"All right. But please be quick, Sapph. If we don't leave soon, we really *are* going to be late." With a brisk nod, Amethyst whisks out of the room, and I'm finally given a moment of peace.

I chuckle as I get dressed. I have to admit, I *do* look the part. The dress—courtesy of the Fae—hugs my figure in all the right places, and the lace pattern at the front reminds me of fresh spring leaves.

I smile at my reflection and head for the door. Outside, Caden is waiting for me.

His eyes widen momentarily as he takes in the outfit. "Wow."

"Yes, back at you."

He looks stunning in a dark suit, black shirt and tie, and polished shoes instead of his usual boots. My breath hitches as his green eyes rake me from head to toe and back again.

"Do we have to go to this thing, Sapph?"

I barely contain a moan, my insides turning molten when he draws me close and presses a kiss to the inside of my wrist, the top of my shoulder, and then the corner of my mouth. "I wish we didn't have to."

Caden pulls back. "I won't tell if you won't." His eyes sparkle. "Seriously, you look gorgeous enough to eat."

I flush under his innuendo, wishing I could take him up on the offer, but shake my head. "Amethyst would literally murder us if we didn't turn up."

He slides an arm around my waist as we make our way outside. "It's a risk I'm willing to take."

"Well." I stand on tiptoe to brush my lips against the edge of his jaw. "I'm not. I've had enough death and destruction for one lifetime, I think."

Caden's expression flickers with amusement. His bare wrist peeks out from the edge of his shirt cuff. My gaze drops to the faint scorch mark there. Before I can dwell on the dark memories that have given me nightmares ever since, his voice pulls me back to the present.

"So, are we taking your car, or my truck?"

"Neither." I smirk at him. "Aveen gave me an amulet as thanks for ending Azriel, and we're using that to get to the Accord Headquarters. Hold onto me, Caden. You're about to go for a ride unlike any you've ever been on. Even better than that motorcycle of yours."

THE RUSH of Fae magic is different to the magic wielded by witches, and it is different again to that wielded by celestials. Caden staggers slightly when we arrive at the entrance to the main hall in the Accord Headquarters building, but to his credit he shakes his head a couple of times and then shoots me a grin.

Strategically stationed Fae staff direct us down myriad corridors to a large ballroom, where the dinner is set to take place. When we enter, the last stragglers are taking their seats at the many round tables dotted throughout the room.

Several heads turn as we weave through the tables, joining Topaz, Amethyst, Kyan and Dane at a large round table reserved for the six of us.

"Got a little lost," I mutter in Topaz's ear as I slide into my seat. "What did we miss?"

"Only Ky and Dane arm wrestling." Topaz rolls her eyes with an affectionate smile. "They nearly broke the table."

I giggle. "Who won?"

"Neither."

When I raise an eyebrow, Topaz glances at my sister.

"Amethyst got sick of it and beat them both to shut them up." She lowers her voice to a whisper. "She used a strength-enhancing charm, which they suspect, but neither of them have worked up the courage to ask her."

I glance around, surprised by the set-up of the room which seems quite different from the last time I was here. There are supes of all kinds—Fae, shifters, witches and warlocks, gremlins, goblins, and vampires, among other species. I expected all of the supes to sit with their own kind, but instead, the small round tables are filled with a mixture of species.

I catch sight of Aveen. He's even paler than usual, and his arm is still in a sling, but at least he's alive. He's listening intently to the man seated next to him, his eyes glittering as he takes a sip of liquid that looks like wine. I realize with a rush of surprise that the other man is Caden's packmate, Patrick.

And I get even more of a shock when Aveen puts down his wine and lays a hand on Patrick's thigh, and the shifter covers the Fae's hand with his own and leaves it there.

"*Whoa.*"

Caden leans toward me, following my line of vision.

"Opposites attract, huh?" he murmurs, smirking at me.

"It's awesome." I look up at him with an answering grin. "I guess that theory worked for us, didn't it?"

"It did, indeed." He does what Aveen just did to Patrick, and lays a warm hand on my thigh.

The place falls silent as a Fae stands up from the long table at the head of the room. The table is full of seated officials in long elegant robes, along with a handful of beings that are unmistakeably celestial, Isiah and Elebeth among them.

The man spreads his arms wide, grinning at the room at large.

"Welcome," he says. "Thank you for coming to the first Accord Summit in more than thirty years. This has been... a long time coming."

A couple of scattered laughs follow, and the man dips his head in acknowledgment of his audience.

"As you all know, the new Accord Agreement has been drawn up by representatives from every species, magical and non-magical." His gaze turns toward the immortal beings sitting at the end of his table, listening politely. "And, this time, we have a celestial representative who has agreed to be one of the signatories. I am honored to announce the celestials will be joining us in our endeavor to make this world a fair and just place, free from tyranny and with equality for all."

Loud applause follows his words.

Isiah stands briefly to acknowledge the crowd's pleasure in the announcement, before sinking into his seat once more. He looks vaguely amused by the whole event, but at least he's here, and willing to sign.

Sitting by his side is Elebeth. I catch her eye and she shoots me a tiny smile, raising her wineglass. It's half empty already.

Still experimenting with human beverages. I guess she's moved on from tea.

"And finally," the Fae man's voice draws my attention once more. "I have to thank several brave individuals for their role in defeating the greatest threat to our world in over a century. The Redferne witches—Sapphire, Amethyst, and Topaz—and the hellhound shifters who stepped up to protect them, Kyan, Dane, and Caden."

The applause is deafening. I duck my head, my cheeks burning, gratified to see that Caden looks just as awkward about the whole thing as I am. When the attention finally leaves us, he leans close and whispers under the guise of tucking a strand of my hair back in place. "We should have run when we had the chance."

I elbow him, trying to focus on what the Accord Council man is saying as we surreptitiously sink further down into our chairs.

"Without their bravery—and particularly that of Sapphire and Caden, who defeated the fallen one—none of us would be sitting here today. And for that reason, I award you, Sapphire and Caden, with the Chains of Aother." The Fae holds up a heavy-looking chain, wrought out of a glowing, silvery material. "The possession of such a gift will grant you both a long and happy life."

We're shoved to our feet, and have to endure another round of applause before we're allowed to sink back into obscurity.

I catch Caden's eye. My stomach flip-flops at the pained expression on his face. Poor guy looks like this is worse than facing down a demon.

"First chance we get," I whisper. "We're out of here."

"A high-stakes escape."

We don't stick around for the rest of the speeches. I quietly arrange for Amethyst to take the Chains of Aother home with her and keep them until I can drop by to retrieve them. She squeezes my arm before I leave, shooting a glance toward Caden. "Take care, sis. Love you."

"Love you too, Ammie."

Topaz and Kyan catch us just before we slip out of the hall. The ceremony is winding down, but the small corridor that leads out of the Headquarters is still pretty empty. Topaz flings her arms around my neck and pulls me close.

"Thank you," she whispers. "For everything. You saved my life. You saved us all."

I hug my cousin tightly, tears pricking in my eyes. My lovely, kind, beautiful cousin. Azriel and his demon Luthor had wanted to drag her soul to the Otherworld. Now, thanks to us, none of them will get the chance to hurt anyone else.

Caden's hand slides into mine, warm and comforting. Together, we fall into step on our way out into the afternoon sunlight, and then I invoke Aveen's charm, whisking us home to the front garden of my cottage with a rush of magic and a few moments of disorientation afterward.

When our heads clear, I raise an eyebrow in Caden's direction.

"Hmm." I tilt my head up at him. "This isn't very high-stakes."

"What are you talking about?" Caden's voice is tinged with amusement, but he's still shaking his head, getting his balance and coordination back.

"I'm just saying... when you mentioned a high-stakes escape, I was expecting a little more excitement."

"Well..." Caden furrows his brow, like he's thinking hard. Then, without warning, he sweeps his arm under my legs and hitches me up. "How's *this* for excitement?"

I squeal breathlessly, kicking my legs in the air.

"What—*Caden!*" I giggle as he jogs up my front path and leaps up the stairs to my front door. He's not even out of breath, the bastard. "Put me down!"

He eventually sets me down outside the door. His hands don't let go of my hips. Instead, he pulls me into him and leans in for a deep kiss that leaves me breathless for an entirely different reason.

"Come on," he rumbles in my ear, and I melt against him. "I've got plans for when we get inside, beautiful witch."

I don't have a sassy comeback for that one. He knows he has me, as surely as the sun rises and sets.

Now, and always.

I wrap my hand in his, holding tight, and settle for, "Let's go in, then, Mister Hellhound. I might have a few plans of my own, for you."

ALSO BY JEN KATEMI

Thank you for reading! I hope you enjoyed *Bewitched in Darkness*, the final book in the *Hellhound Protectors* series.

If so, please consider leaving a review.

Now you've read the *Hellhound Protectors* trilogy, there is a whole new series to enjoy.

The *Blood Fae Chronicles* is set in the same world and features banshee-human hybrid sisters, Aleah, Indigo and Maewen Jones, and their fight to save both the human world and the Winter Court of Faerie.

Suggested reading order:

Banshee Cry

Banshee Song

Banshee Power

Banshee Quest: Renna's Curse (prequel and sequel in one).

For a full list of titles by Jen Katemi, visit:

www.JenKatemi.com/books

ABOUT THE AUTHOR

Jen Katemi is a *USA Today* bestselling author of steamy contemporary and paranormal romance. She is published with Evernight Publishing, and previously as Jennifer Lynne with Red Sage. Jen also has forged a successful indie career including her popular BLOOD FAE CHRONICLES, GODS OF LOVE, and FORBIDDEN series.

When she's not writing, Jen runs an editing and proofreading service, looks after the family, and pampers various cats. She lives in Melbourne, Australia.

Sign up to receive new release email notifications, at her website:

www.JenKatemi.com